The Subtle Dance of Impulse and Light

The Subtle Dance of Impulse and Light:

A Collection of Episodes

Brett Riley

INK
BRUSH
PRESS

ISBN: 978-0-9888632-0-0
Library of Congress Control Number: 2013932625

Manufactured in the United States

Ink Brush Press
Temple and Dallas

As always, for Kalene (who is
most certainly not Carol)
and for Shauna, Brendan, and Maya
for their continued inspiration

Fiction from Ink Brush Press

Laurie Champion, ed., *Texas Told'em*

Terry Dalrymple, *Fishing for Trouble*

Terry Dalrymple, ed., *Texas Soundtrack*

Andrew Geyer, *Dixie Fish*

Andrew Geyer, *Siren Songs from the Heart of Austin*

H. Palmer Hall, *Into the Thicket*

Dave Kuhne, *The Road to Roma*

Myra McLarey, *The Last Will and Testament of Rosetta Sugars Tramble*

Eric Muirhead, *Cab Tales*

Brett Riley, *The Subtle Dance of Impulse and light*

Jim Sanderson, *Faded Love*

Jim Sanderson, *Dolph's Team*

Melvin Sterne, *Zara*

Dan Williams, *The Lords of Leftovers*

For information on these and other IBP books, go to

www.inkbrushpress.com

Acknowledgments

I always say that writing is a solitary profession until it isn't. In that regard, I would like to thank God, without Whom nothing is possible. Thanks to Kalene Westmoreland, always my first reader and editor; to Jerry Craven and the staff of Ink Brush Press, for all their hard work; to Jamie Brown, Mallory Young, and Bill Church, who believed in these stories before anyone else; and to my family, friends, and readers, without whom I would be just another grumpy guy muttering to himself in a dark room.

I am grateful to the editors of *The Broadkill Review* and *The Mochila Review* for publishing some of the stories in this collection.

CONTENTS

1   An Anecdote

9   Dated

19   The Security System

29   Just Because You're Paranoid

39   Doesn't Mean They Aren't Out to Get You

51   I Know This Guy, See?

69   It's All in the Reflexes

81   A Theatrical Evening

93   The Handy Helper

109   The Classroom

123   House Arrest

135   Phone Tag

147   Travel Plans

161   Lights, Action

An Anecdote

I learned everything I know about love from watching *Die Hard* movies. Maybe that's why all my problems seem to have happened to me before, like a trite plot point in a shoot-em-up movie. You might think I'm kidding, so let me tell you a story. It's what I do, after all. I'm a writer. In my profession we call this kind of tale an anecdote. Here goes.

My girlfriend Carol loves to drive over to Crossett on weekends and walk in the park. She loves it. Every Saturday, even if it rains, she shows up and makes me drive twenty miles just to stroll under pine trees, which we could have done in the woods behind my house. She kneels down and makes chirpy noises at the squirrels and laughs at kids as they zoom down the old faded-silver slide, the one that stands about ten feet tall and looks as if its surface has been polished smooth by whole generations of kiddie asses in short pants and scratchy new blue jeans. Me, I mostly concentrate on keeping my underwear out of my ass crack. Squirrels and kids? I've seen them, and they didn't particularly impress me the first time.

Not that I dislike squirrels and kids. I don't. It's just that I'd rather stay home and watch a football game in my favorite robe and an old pair of boxers. Instead, I find myself in Crossett of all places, sweating and itching and breathing the dysentery-fart stench of the paper mill, watching Carol make googly expressions at somebody's baby. That park is filled with people we don't know and will never see again—unless it's in the goddam park. Who needs it?

Now, everything I've said so far is what writers call the exposition, which is kind of like the pre-game show you have to watch before kickoff. Now we're getting to the meat of the anecdote I promised you, so pay attention.

One Saturday I woke up and realized that I had finally had enough.

I had slept in a weird position the night before, so my neck felt like an ADHD-afflicted two-year-old had tied my spine in a bow. My head pounded; my legs felt weak. I had no desire to step outside, not even long enough to walk down the drive and check the mail. Plus, Arkansas was playing on channel seven. I don't mean Arkansas State, either, or Arkansas Tech or Central Arkansas or Southern Arkansas or the University of Arkansas at Little Rock, Pine Bluff, or Monticello. And I damn sure don't mean Parkview's own University of Southeast Arkansas Confederates, who went 1-11 last year with a perfect losing record in the conference. I mean the Hogs, the Razorbacks, the one nationally ranked team in the state.

The opening kickoff was still in the air when Carol walked in, as if she had been standing outside my front door and peeking in the window, just waiting for that moment. She was wearing her cute little blue jogging shorts and a tight t-shirt with a sports bra underneath, like she had entered us into a marathon and had forgotten to tell me. She said

Hey, it's a beautiful day. Why don't you get off the couch, and we'll go to the park.

Just like that, like it's a request, when we both knew it was a demand, an expectation, a call to goddam duty. Trying to ignore the crackling in my neck, I just glanced at her and nodded at the TV set, as if that's all the answer I intended to give and all she should have needed. I was drawing a line in the sand, and I expected her to cross it with her claws out or take the hint and back off. But she just looked at me like a spider was hanging out of my nose and said

What? It's just some ball game. You can watch a ball game any time.

This is how she thinks. Never mind that I love football, and that I only go to the park to shut her up. Never mind that I was propped up on the perfect number of pillows, which I had spent half an hour arranging for maximum comfort and support. Never mind that I was wearing my favorite pair of boxers and had already drunk just enough beer to assure that I'd have to pee behind some tree, probably flanked by a couple of squirrels and a kid eating ice cream. It was just a game that meant nothing to her, so it shouldn't have meant anything to me, either. But it did. So I said

No, it is not just a ball game. This happens to be Arkansas versus the University of Tennessee, two top-15 teams, meaning this game has national championship implications. Jobs are on the line here. The dreams of young men hang in the balance. Millions of bowl dollars could be at stake.

Plus, I'm comfy.

She looked at me like I had just squished and eaten the spider hanging out of my nose and said

Well, you could record it, so

and I interrupted

Not only that, but I can't watch a game any time. You can only see any game once and then it might as well be gone forever. Unlike certain movies and TV and books, games actually happen in real life and you can't re-create the genesis of their truth. Besides, there are only a dozen games per team

and of course she interrupted my lesson on the philosophical implications of football and said

Oh, come off it. They aren't curing cancer. They're running into each other and kicking a ball around

and so by God I interrupted her and said

Besides, if I tape it somebody's just gonna tell me the score and ruin the whole thing. That always happens. Why don't you just grab a beer and a sandwich and sit down? I'll teach you all about the play action pass and the Cover Two.

She put her hand on her hip and cocked her left eyebrow, her gesture that indicates she is dealing with a brain-dead Neanderthal. I ignored her. After a minute or so she said

I don't care about play action passes or the Cover Two. For all I know, you just made that stuff up. I care about going to the park, getting some exercise, spending time together like a real couple

so I came back with

Why do we always do what you want and call it spending time together, and never do what I want because you aren't interested? Can't I be not interested in going to goddam Crossett?

She didn't say anything for a minute, so when Tennessee had to call an early timeout, I turned to look at her. Her pale blue eyes were moist, her lips compressed into a pale thin line. She wasn't crying, but she was close; I had seen that expression before. I only wanted to make a strong point that she would have to consider, one that would at least buy me a little more couch time before I had to haul myself to the bedroom and find a clean pair of pants. But I had really hurt her feelings. I softened my voice and said

Look, honey, I just want to bum around and watch this game. I'd

3

love it if you'd stay. Come on, what do you say?

Now, understand that I figured she would either try to do something I like for once, or she'd pout and I could just pretend that she wasn't there. But no, those options would be too easy and too normal and too sane. Instead she cleared her throat and said

Michael, I will not be prioritized this way. I will not come in second to football. Either you come with me to feed the squirrels or you don't expect me to come back and ask you again.

Now, before I tell you what happened next, I have to admit that I wasn't thinking clearly at the time. I had gotten through three beers already, and secretly I was just trying to hear the game. I doubt I would have burst into laughter if I had really been listening. But the choice she was asking me to make—her and a bunch of squirrels or my new 60-inch flat-screen HDTV and the Hogs—seemed so absurd that I did a spit-take, spewing beer all over the coffee table and shooting it up my nose. It was like something out of a bad sitcom, one where people laugh at things that aren't funny and make jokes that no one gets. Worse, the alcohol in my sinus cavity burned my eyes, making them water so badly that I couldn't see the game or Carol anymore. But I was still laughing, even though my nose felt like someone had shoved a blowtorch up both nostrils. I couldn't help it.

A few seconds later, I heard the door slam. I staggered around, my vision blurred from the tears and pain and laughter, barely able to find the front door, and by the time I got out to the driveway, her Lexus was turning the corner, nearly obliterating a dog and a kid on a tricycle. I stood in the drive, the concrete rough and warm under my bare feet, watching the kid ride like hell back toward his own house, where, as a general rule, crazy women probably didn't try to mow him down with expensive cars. After a few moments, my eyes cleared, and I went back inside, where I eased back down on my pillows and watched the rest of the game. I wished I'd caught her, but I figured, oh well, she'll get over it. It's just one measly trip to the park, right?

But she didn't get over it. She refused to answer the phone for the rest of the weekend. On Monday, I called again. This time, instead of her usual voicemail message, I heard an ear-splitting beep, and then an apologetic but firm female voice said

I'm sorry, but you have dialed a number that is no longer in service. Please hang up and dial your number again.

4

So I did. Same result.

She had changed her number. I shit you not. It was even an unlisted number, so I couldn't talk the 411 people into giving it to me.

I went to her house; she wouldn't come to the door, no matter how long I knocked. She wouldn't reply to any email I sent. And when I showed up at her office on Thursday, she threatened to call the cops and yelled for her partner to grab the mace and stun gun, so I got the hell out of there. As far as I know, she's never owned either of those things, but why take the chance?

When all my friends ask me what happened between us that week, I tell them that she got pissed at me because I didn't want to go feed the squirrels. They laugh and shake their heads. Some of them wink, as if to say, women—whaddya gonna do? We all know what that's like. They're my friends and they mean well, so I let them talk.

But that anecdote doesn't really show you the truth, not all of it anyway.

I left out the fact that Carol and I fought once every few days, usually because of me. In the first weeks after that new TV was delivered (thirty-five bucks added to the purchase price, before taxes), I tended to ignore her so that I could watch sports—football, baseball, hockey, women's figure skating, curling, street luge, anything at all. I could stare at the screen for hours without moving, answering even her most complex questions with mmm hmmmm and nuh uh.

So after a dozen fights about that subject, we came to an agreement. On Saturdays we'd do whatever she wanted, and on Sundays I could watch TV hassle-free. What an arrangement—egalitarian, balanced, *quid pro quo*. I get something, she gets something. But it didn't last.

One Saturday, *Die Hard* ran on HBO. The *Die Hard* series is one of my guilty pleasures—hardly examples of cinematic artistry, often illogical, fairly mindless, and one hell of a lot of fun. Naturally I didn't want to go to the park that day, so we had our first post-agreement disagreement. And over the next weeks, we had more, each with its own catalyst—a John Wayne marathon, some Braves games on WTBS, and a couple of non-televised pick-up basketball games at my friend Dray's house. Always my fault, always because I couldn't hold up my end of a perfectly acceptable arrangement, usually because I wanted to watch my new TV.

How can I explain it? Bruce Willis diving over the side of a skyscraper, a fire hose wrapped around his waist, his wifebeater undershirt

5

soiled and bloody. The crowd rising in unison as Chipper Jones drives a pitch high over the right field wall, the ecstasy of the fan who catches the homer by reaching over a sea of flailing arms, the calm and studious absence of expression on Jones's face as he trots around the bases. John Wayne staring down Lee Marvin in an Old West restaurant, while in the background Jimmy Stewart crouches on the floor over a dirty steak and scattered fried potatoes. Some things you just need to see on a big screen. Size is American.

I guess the Arkansas-Tennessee game was, in the end, too much to ask for. I refused to go to the park. I watched the game alone. And Carol, having finally had enough, simply erased me from her life, like a channel you lock out of your television so your kids can't watch it after you go to sleep. We got back together a few weeks later; we usually do. But now when Carol surfs through the images of her life and comes to those weeks, she skips over the memory of me, as if I had winked out of existence for a time. How many hours, days, weeks were lost because of a college football game? And if you added it with all the other losses, how much time would you have? What did we lose in those weeks that we can never get back? What did we miss entirely?

But at least I had *Die Hard* and its sequels, a quartet of films that taught me about the bonds between men and women. John McClane always gets the girl, no matter how badly he's fucked up. Problem: your wife moves across the country to pursue her career, and you refuse to support the decision. Solution: show her you're a he-man stud who's still sensitive enough to admit that you love her, in this case by killing several gun-toting high-tech thieves and walking on glass in your bare feet. Problem: a rogue elite military unit is using your wife and her fellow airline passengers as pawns in their own dastardly scheme. Solution: terminate the mercs and save several hundred people. Problem: you are being stalked by another set of high-tech thieves, who are out to use your escapades as a diversion so they can steal a lot of gold. Solution: kill all these thieves, too, while saving truckloads of civilians and solving America's racism problem. And as for the fourth one, *Live Free or Die Hard*—well, I remember liking it at the time, but now I don't remember a goddam thing about it. Not one thing. So what did I learn?

In the first two films, McClane gets the girl. In *Die Hard with a Vengeance*, the girl does not appear, but we do learn that McClane has lost her again because he's an asshole. In the end, though, he calls her, thus taking the first step, reestablishing contact, being the sensitive he-man again. You know that things will turn out fine. And if they don't—if, say, he's divorced in part four—well, by then he'll have a kid to worry about. He'll be the sensitive father, misunderstood but ultimately loved.

I keep trying to play that ending in my own life. I act selfishly or thoughtlessly, and I figure if I'm masculine, tough, uncompromising, and impenetrable, I can do pretty much whatever I want. And if I lose the girl, I can always get her back in time for the sequel.

But sometimes, after I borrow some change from my sidekick and try to apologize for whatever it is that I've done this time, no one answers the phone. Sometimes I think Bruce Willis has betrayed me, that I've trusted too much in someone else's construction of the world. Sometimes I think that real life has no relationship at all to the movies and to TV shows like *Gilligan's Island*. No relationship to the stories we tell. Every day that all the Carols I've ever known don't call me back, every time they refuse to let me in their offices long enough to say I'm sorry, I feel like my life is a movie with no director, a story by an author who doesn't know how things are going to end.

Dated

Not long ago, my editor called me at home, and soon my agent beeped in on the other line. Neither one of them would go away, so I switched to conference call mode and we spent the next two hours discussing my latest book, a fictionalized first-person account of how my technophobia affects my love life. Some people in my circle hate the idea, probably afraid that I'll make them too easily recognizable, but I'm beginning to doubt I'll ever finish it anyway. You see, I've become obsessed with re-telling *The Scarlet Letter* from the perspective of Hester's vagina. You know, to finally acknowledge the story's true narrative center. My editor was saying

Mike, if you write that book

he meant the one about technology

it will stop selling almost immediately because whatever technology you write into it will already be obsolete by the time we launch. The world's moving too fast for a book like this. It will become dated.

I didn't believe that he was right, not even close, so I said

Hardly. I'm not really writing about technology, Morrie. I'm writing about love.

Dated implies that my subject matter and/or themes will be so particular to one time period that the work won't interest audiences of later eras. I don't happen to believe in dated work, so I wasn't terribly concerned about how the book might sell. Instead, I envisioned the opening scene of my newest project, wherein I planned to describe Hester's vagina, every wrinkle and fold and infected pubic hair. Hey, people weren't exactly clean back then, right? Plus, it would be the first time in history that the audience gets into Hester's pants, not counting that crappy Demi Moore film. But I couldn't really concentrate on the image, because my editor said

If you tie all your stories together with technology that is specific to a specific time, how will people relate to the book in five years? Hell, how will they relate next month, when everything you're writing about has been replaced? I mean

My phone beeped again as Morrie continued to dissect my approach, so I took the opportunity to ignore him, checking my caller ID display. It said

UNAVAILABLE

which usually means telemarketer or bill collector. I don't answer those calls unless I'm really bored, so I let the phone beep. It fragmented Morrie's lecture. He said

And further, this topic could affect BEEP-BEEP markets because those people don't even have all this BEEP-BEEP you're talking about.

His voice had become part human and part machine, a cyborg voice right out of a Jim Cameron film, even as he tried to deconstruct a project on the juxtaposition of art and technology. Some might call that ironic. Me, I just thought it was funny.

After the beeping stopped I pretended to listen again, but of course I was busy with mentally writing the new *Scarlet Letter*. I decided that I'd actually need to write a prequel, a book that ended with Pearl's birth. The real untold story. Otherwise, Hester's vagina would remain locked up in two hundred layers of Puritan undergarment and would therefore have little to say about anything but coarse fabrics and crotch-rotting humidity.

Meanwhile, Morrie was saying

Damn it Mike I don't even think you're listening

and I said

Sure I am. I just don't agree. I still say love is the eternal theme. The technology motif will function as a window into this historical moment. A lot of great books have been written about subjects that don't directly apply to other times, and they still get read because their themes never get old

and Morrie said

A lot of books, huh? Name one.

Darlene, my agent, chimed in with

Moby-Dick

and I echoed

Moby-Dick. There you go. A great American Novel, and what is it about? Whaling. Sperm oil. Today most people probably think that's some kind of lubricant. And plotwise, not a lot happens in *Moby-Dick*. But the book has lasted because it's also about good and evil, and obsession, and man's depravity, and the unknowable nature of nature. People still read it, Morrie

and Darlene said

Damn right. Well said, Mike

and Morrie said

Darlene, I think you've forgotten that you work on commission. You might make fifty bucks on this book, and yet you sit there defending it. I'm trying to help you, Mike. I want your books to sell now and let the next hundred and fifty years take care of themselves

and Darlene broke in with

What about his literary reputation, Morrie? Huh? He wants to sell, sure. I want him to sell. But he's already made us a lot of money, and he isn't some hack who'll crank out formulaic junk for us at the same time every year. Sometimes he's got to write what he feels

and I liked that, so I said

Hell, if Melville were alive, he'd be writing this book

which I knew would piss Morrie off, and it did, so he said

Don't flatter yourself, Mike. And remember, Melville died broke and clinically depressed.

Before I could say anything else, Darlene snapped

Now hold on a minute, Morrie. You just back off

and I stopped listening. Perhaps I'd call my prequel *The Scarlet Labia*. Morrie would hate it, so I would have to win over Darlene. Of course, she might hate it even worse, since she had already chided me about my allegedly one-dimensional and perhaps misogynistic portrayal of women. I never really understood that. I don't hate women; I just sometimes write about men who do. Goddam critics—I hear Hemingway felt the same way about them.

Anyway, while Morrie and Darlene shouted at each other, I decided that the vagina would have to function as a tightly constructed metaphor for sensuality, femaleness though not necessarily femininity, and secularism. Dimmesdale's cock, especially at the moment of coition, would stand for patriarchy, the rigid social code of Puritanism, and the hazy metaphysical debates of the time. Sex, the meeting of these two opposing states, would represent the space of being human, the merger of poles, a transcendental humanism that Emerson would have applauded. I would, in other words, commit a minor literary sin by constructing a modern-day allegory based on a nineteenth-century Romance. Even worse, I'd take it seriously.

Morrie and Darlene were still going at it. Morrie was saying

You're supposed to take his side; you're his agent. But one would think that you'd also be worried about your own bottom line

and Darlene snorted and said

We just went through this. Mike has sold more books this year than any other so-called serious writer on your list. I think that you got gun-shy after you okayed that latest Digby Darrymore clunker

and Morrie immediately barked

Do not start that again. Do not disparage the Darrymore book. It will be considered a masterpiece of postmodern fiction in fifty years. He's a genius misunderstood by the public of his time

and Darlene broke in with

Now wait just a cotton-picking minute. I didn't know you could read the future. And besides, you just told Mike that you wanted to worry about the present and let the future take care of itself. Now you're yammering about how well the book will sell long after you're dead. So which is it, Morrie?

and Morrie came back with

I'd rather the Darrymore book sell now, sure, but at least I firmly believe that it will sell at some point

and Darlene said

The Darrymore book is a doorstop, a paperweight, a cure for insomnia.

My phone beeped at me again. I almost didn't notice. I had decided to focus my first few chapters on Hester's upbringing and was sketching an outline on an old pizza box I had left on the coffee table, making sure to write around the damp grease stains. Given the Puritans' penchant for sexual prudery and biological determinism, I figured that Hester's vagina —the physical seat of her sexuality—should be born to victimhood. Therefore, the first chapters should explore the vagina's imprisonment beneath Hester's garments and its emotional angst at being blamed for all the evil in the world. Such an opening would make a nice parallel to the beginning of *The Scarlet Letter*, the scenes after The Custom House in which Hester and Pearl emerge from jail. I figured the first act of my book could end with Hester's accidental discovery of her clitoris and the subsequent liberation, so to speak, of the vagina as a whole. I intended to make young Hester a chronic masturbator, if only to annoy certain critics who swear I only define my female characters by their physicality.

With little more on my mind than the joys and subversive nature of self-love, I checked my caller ID. It read

UNAVAILABLE

and I was going to ignore it again, but Morrie and Darlene were still arguing the merits of Digby's book, a twelve-hundred-page study of one hour in the life of a bus driver and his sentient belly button lint. I didn't really care to hear any more about that kind of self-indulgent shit, so I pushed the button and said

Hello

and a voice said

Good evening. May I speak with Mr. Seymour?

The voice sounded like a ray of pure sunshine. This guy had rehearsed his ass off. I could respect that, so I said

Sure, can I ask who's calling?

and the voice said

My name is Irv. I'm calling on behalf of Powerful Products Productions, Incorporated. Am I speaking with Mr. Seymour?

and I said

Sure are, Irv. What can I do for you?

and Irv said

Mr. Seymour, I'm prepared to offer you a wonderful opportunity tonight, one that is both affordable and practical. Powerful Products Productions offers discount prices on specialized items that you simply can't find anywhere else. Today's featured item is a combination potato peeler/alarm clock, convenient for your kitchen or your bedside table. For only four easy payments of $27.95, you can own this

and I broke in with

Wait, wait, wait. Hold on a second, Irv. Are you telling me that someone has finally made it convenient to wake up at, say, 5:46 AM and peel a shitload of potatoes without even getting out of bed?

and Irv said

That's correct, Mr. Seymour, up to five pounds before the peelings have to be cleared

and I interrupted

This is fantastic, Irv. Do you have any idea how long I've been waiting for this? Years, Irv, decades, my whole life. Oh, the bunches, the bags, the sheer billions of potatoes that I plan to peel in my bed

and Irv, sounding a tad confused, said

Uh, right. So if I can just have your credit card number

and I interrupted

Now see here, Irv. First things are definitely first. Before I give you my credit card number, answer me this: what do you think of a prequel to Hawthorne's Romantic novel *The Scarlet Letter*, told from the perspective of Hester's vagina?

After a long pause, Irv said

Uh, well, I, uh, think it's a bad idea to retool a classic, and frankly, a thinking sexual organ seems a bit perverse

so I said

You're a fucking asshole, Irv. Don't ever call me again or I'll sue you for harassment. And by the way, anybody selling potato peeler alarm clocks over the phone should never use the sentence I think it's a bad idea. Goodbye

and Irv said

But

but I had already hung up.

After that conversation I needed to pee, and as I was standing at the toilet I decided that I would create a few scenes in which a teenaged Hester would masturbate in the woods while several Puritan boys look on. The boys would be in hiding, of course, but Hester would know they were there, and she'd get off on it. This exploration of her exhibitionist tendencies should resonate in Hawthorne's work; I'll be foreshadowing her sensuality, her ability to stand up under scrutinizing gazes, and the love of nature that she passes on to her elf-child.

After I shook off, I decided that I should check in on Morrie and Darlene. I put the phone back to my ear just in time to hear Morrie say

—don't know anything about art that lasts. I'm telling you, *Elbow Lisp* will be a classic. It will be debated by critics and studied in English programs in universities across the world.

It occurred to me that Digby's book was already being debated by at least two people, but I didn't say anything because Darlene snickered and said

Well, if a twelve-hundred-page study of belly button lint is a classic, then everyone in academia is insane, so it won't really matter to me.

I thought that was really funny, so I laughed, and the sound of my voice reminded them that I had once been part of a conversation about my own book. I considered hanging up on them and calling my girlfriend, Carol, but then I remembered that she had broken up with me after I watched six straight days of Wimbledon coverage on my new satellite system and that I hadn't been able to get her new unlisted number yet. Or was the argument about a ball game? Or maybe hockey?

And as I sifted through the memories of all the fights I'd ever had with my longtime girlfriend, I began wondering, as I often did, what it would be like to sleep with Darlene. She's got red hair the color of cartoon fire, pale skin peppered with freckles and ominous varicose veins like purple starbursts on her left calf, a pointy nose made less for breathing than for poking unknown lovers in the eye, pale green eyes set in whites perpetually bloodshot, breath smelling faintly of Listerine and Absolut. I have only met her in person a handful of times, our other business conducted through telephone and email and fax and video conferencing and instant messages, and still I wonder what she smells like in the middle of the night, what her first words of the day might sound like.

But I never ask because of Carol. Even when we've split up, we're always on the verge of reconciliation, as if our mutual romantic developments got arrested in ninth grade. If I ever actually slept with Darlene and Carol found out, it would be over for good, and what the hell would I do then? Besides, Darlene and I have the best kind of relationship—flirtatious, protective, electronic. No deep feelings, no bodily fluids, no his and hers sock drawers. Black-and-whiteness of paper, pixilated images. Plus, she's married to Morrie, who could probably make real trouble for me, professionally speaking. Anyway, after I laughed, she shrieked

You see? You see? Mike knows. He knows the difference between postmodern high art and nonsensical mumbo-jumbo

and I got a bit nervous because, like I just said, Morrie could make my life miserable. So I said

Well, now, I wouldn't go that far. I think Digby lays it on a bit thick and pretentious, but I wouldn't necessarily call it mumbo-jumbo

so Morrie said

Ah-ha. Mike isn't as on your side as you think

and Darlene said

That's not what he said

and by this time I was scared. I needed both these people on my side.

So I decided to turn the conversation back to its original topic—me. I said

Listen, can we forget about Digby's lint and get back to my book? I mean, how long do I have to sit here and listen to you two debate some other author's merits?

I could hear Morrie slapping his forehead as he said

Jesus, Mike, you're right. I'm sorry, man

and Darlene mumbled

Yeah

so I said

No problem. Morrie, my book will not be dated. It won't. And even if it doesn't age well, the world won't end. It's what I want to say

although I didn't really know if that were true or not, but Morrie said

Well, look, you're the writer. But I just want to express my reservations.

He kept on talking, but I was suddenly thinking of Dimmesdale's penis, wondering if I should give it a voice, too. I know that a lot of critics would say that any work by a male writer represents the voice of the penis, but I think that's pretty unfair. I considered that maybe I should make the novel a sort of dialogue, narrated in alternating chapters by the penis and the vagina, the better to explore Dimmesdale's character and to set up a metaphor for problems and issues in gender relations. On the other hand, I also thought that perhaps such an approach would prove too broad and difficult, in terms of both structure and scope. I didn't want the book to collapse under its own weight, like *Elbow Lisp*. The pizza box's dry surfaces had been consumed with outlined material, so I made a mental note to myself to make a note to myself.

But really, I was tired of talking, tired of listening to Morrie and Darlene yammer. All these words they were throwing around weren't writing my story. So when Darlene said

not something I see as feasible within the next year, right, Mike?

I said

Um, well, actually I'm not sure at the moment, and I'm going to have to finish this later because um well my stomach. I'm feeling nauseous, gonna run and take some Dramamine or something and lie down, sorry so quick, bye

and Darlene said

But

but I hung up. I slumped down into the deep cushions of my couch, left ear throbbing, my neck muscles pulsing. I turned the television to a preview channel and searched for a ball game. Thirty-minute increments of time shaped into neat colored rectangles of organization, each channel scrolling up and off the screen too fast to note. I wondered if Morrie and Darlene would stop for take-out on the way to their house in the Hamptons, where the water would be too cold for a swim, where they would probably make love in front of a fireplace on expensive rugs and later talk about Michael Seymour and his lunatic ideas about art, of the southern writer's roomy house in southeast Arkansas where nothing ever happened except a kind of life that they probably think only exists in stories by Faulkner and Welty and where surely nothing could inspire books that would reach farther than their cell phones and email blind carbon copies, little dreaming that I planned to unleash upon the world a book full of talking sexual organs, a book of thinking perversities that would offend telemarketers named Irv, a book in which everything has a voice but only an illusion of agency because the future was long ago determined by fate, biology, or Hawthorne's Romantic Puritanism.

My phone rang again, just as I found a college basketball game on a regional network affiliate. It rang twelve times, but I had decided to be unavailable.

The Security System

What I'm about to tell you might be considered a Once upon a Time story, but believe me, it's no fairy tale. One day I was raking leaves in my backyard, just trying to keep busy, working my muscles to clear my head. Earlier, awakening from a light nap, I had suddenly felt sure that every mechanical device I owned—electric, gas, solar—had been designed to confuse me so that I would always need the government and Big Oil to help me understand the world. Paranoid, yes, but also quite conceivable. I had immersed myself too deeply in machines, toaster ovens and microfridges and wristwatches that could keep time in sixteen different ways. I needed a low-tech physical activity, an instrument other than my cell phone or laptop. That rake and its long metallic fingers represented my grip on actuality, the banal earthiness of the task my elixir.

I had been raking for over an hour, excavating narrow trails of grass. Rhythmically, mechanically, I liberated them, brown giving way to pale yellow, as if the leaves were a coverlet I was turning down. The crisp air burned my lungs and sinuses, my paranoia bleeding into deep serenity.

I was still raking when my girlfriend Carol pulled into my driveway, the breeze from her two-year-old cornflower blue Saturn kicking leaves into temporary flights of spiraling elegance. She worked in Pinedale and had driven the fifteen miles to my house in Parkview without calling ahead, which meant that something was wrong. Unless she was mad or trying to catch me doing something wrong, Carol was a call-before-coming-over kind of woman. She opened the door of the car and swung out her left leg, paused, appeared to search for something in her purse. I could see her face but not her expression, her finely tuned and deeply tanned calf and shin but not the little patch of fine blonde hairs that her razor always missed down near her ankle, the left foot in a pair of

19

fashionable flats too distant to reveal color, only possibilities obscured by distance and tricks of the afternoon light.

She stepped out of the car, flats—navy blue? black? some deep, rich green?—crunching across the gravel in the drive, whispering through the grass, rasping through the leaves not yet raked. Every footfall brought her closer, brought her haziness into sharper and sharper relief. Her shoes were black, her blonde ankle hairs gossamer transparent, her expression a furrowed-brow wrinkled-nose set-teeth grimace of perturbation. And this last detail eliminated any surprise I might have felt when she cocked her fist, stepped forward with her black-flat-encased right foot, pivoted at the hip to gather force, and punched me in the nose as hard as she could.

She was still wearing the platinum-studded-with-diamonds ring I had given her. I watched curiously as her fist came toward me surprisingly slowly, shards of light bouncing off the ring, the tiny wrinkles crisscrossing her knuckles looming larger and larger. When the fist made contact I could feel the metal's cold bite, the diamond's unforgiving solidity; bright reds and blues exploded behind my eyelids. I fell straight back into a pile of leaves that sighed as it received me, a raspy back-of-the-throat whisper of protest and acquiescence.

My nose sang white heat and dripped bloody snot, and I heard Carol's voice, fading with the distance as she walked back to her car, each new word farther away than the last. She said

That's for what happened Saturday, you asshole.

I know what happened Saturday. But before Saturday there was three weeks ago, when I first got the idea for the security system. I was playing basketball with my best friend Dray, an exercise in futility since Dray stands 6'5". He wore sweats, even though the temperature hovered in the mid-70s, a half-moon patch of perspiration under each arm. As usual, he was dominating me, and I was unsuccessfully trying to throw him off his game by discussing work and my love life. I crouched low to the ground and dribbled the ball with my right hand, shuffling forward as I said

I think the government is monitoring my alcohol purchases, so I'm writing a story about it.

Dray reached out with one of his freakish scarecrow arms and swatted the ball away from me. Before I realized that I had lost possession, he was driving to the basket. Two steps away, he picked up his dribble and soared through the air, dunking the ball with both hands. The bastard. He said

Jesus, Mike, are you still on that paranoid trip? You think everything's a conspiracy. News flash—nobody cares that much about you. By the way, that's game

and I said

Yes, I know that's game. You make me sick, you tall skinny fuck.

Dray laughed and said

Anyway, let's assume for a second that somebody wants to track you. Fine. But why would the government care how much vodka and wine you drink?

and I said

Who can figure out why they do what they do? All I know is that those receipts list too much information—what you buy, when you buy it, how you pay, from exactly which store, your credit card number. And the register prints a store copy, too

so Dray said

It makes no sense to me, especially if you use cash. How can they trace the purchase then?

and I came back with

Surveillance tapes and the receipts. A simple cross-reference of camera time and receipt time.

Dray shook his head and said

Well, I can't see Wilbur's Liquor as a government front. Say, what did you get Carol for her birthday?

And at this point the sensation hit me, the one every stupid unthinking forgetful lugnut feels when he realizes that he has completely forgotten his girlfriend's birthday. I'm talking about the same woman who once, and for no particular reason, showed up with a new police scanner just for gathering story ideas and a leather duster both for keeping warm and looking cool and a triple layer chocolate cake and two pints of vanilla ice cream and a case of bottled beer and five of the lugnut's closest friends. The same woman who cried when he forgot the two-month anniversary of the first time he actually undid her bra without irreparably bending a clasp, the same woman who would be twice as angry to learn that his best friend had remembered and was therefore possibly a better candidate for life partner. The sensation feels like being kicked square in the crotch by a horse. And my feelings must have been obvious because Dray said

You forgot, didn't you? Jesus, Mike, even I remembered. What kind of a stupid unthinking forgetful lugnut are you?

which is where I got the metaphor I plagiarized above. I gave Dray the finger. He smirked, the bastard. I took the ball and dribbled aimlessly, hoping the staccato rhythm would help me think. Dray pulled up a lawn chair and sat down, sipped a bottle of water, watched me. I searched the dusty underside of memory, hoping for a word, a picture, a fragment of an image, anything that would spark an idea. But all I could think of was the last receipt I got at Wilbur's, a small rectangular piece of white paper proving that I had purchased one case of Shiner Bock, one pint of Jose Cuervo, and a bottle of Absolut. At 5:26:07 PM on 9/17/10. Using VISA, #XXXX XXXX XXXX 1026. I wondered what the register tape would show—all sixteen numbers, obviously, a code permitting entry into my life, my finances, my innermost alcoholic fantasies, and who knows where the register tape goes, probably right to the government or my own personal CIA hitman, and I might have gone right on dribbling that basketball on the court of my own paranoia if Dray hadn't said

Hey, man, how about a security system?

So, you see, everything that happened was really Dray's fault. He said the words security system and reminded me of Carol's own phobia—burglars. I had no direct knowledge of its root, but I knew it existed. Every night after crawling in bed, fluffing her pillow, settling in under the covers and the central air, she would get up anywhere from two to six times, and always for the same reason—to check the locks. On occasion as she was settling back in bed, managing somehow to pull the covers completely off of me, I'd say

Carol, that door has not magically unlocked itself in the last two minutes. You're obsessive-compulsive. They have medication for that

and she would usually say

I'm not obsessive-compulsive. I'm thorough and safety-conscious

to which I once replied

Oh, and I don't suppose you're in denial either. You're just self-analytical and always right

but only once because the resulting fight lasted longer than the ritual.

So when Dray—that bastard—suggested a security system, I thought, *Voila*. A perfect gift. Carol can stay in bed, and I can get more sleep.

The concept, of course, was absurd. When I was working on my MFA down at LSU, I was one of approximately 30,000 students, around three times the population of Parkview and Pinedale combined. Parkview employed perhaps seven or eight city cops, most of whom generally sat either in gas stations drinking coffee or in their cars, bored, trying to trap speeders. Not exactly a hotbed of criminal activity.

Even so, the town had a security firm. At least that's what some people called it. Others called it Big Edna's Window Tinting, Automotive Care, and Security Systems. Mostly, Big Edna changed locks or installed stronger doors. But most people in town don't have my kind of money, so I hired Edna to build a real system at Carol's house—security doors, stronger window locks and steel bars on the outside, electronic alarm with keypad combination, motion detectors, everything connected to the guard-house, which doubled as the home of one John R. Cowell, an out-of-work bicycle repairman whom Edna recommended. I hired him, at three hundred dollars a week, to be Carol's personal guard. I had never met Mr. John R. Cowell, but I needed somebody. The cops in Parkview wouldn't put down their free Gas Mart coffee and donuts for little things like burglary or breaking and entering, and the real security firms would have to drive two hours just to reach her place.

Big Edna assured me that John R. Cowell, an ex-Marine, remembered all his training in self-defense and weaponry. Apparently he had no social life to speak of, meaning that he would always be home to answer the alarm. She also promised to look for a second guard, since Mr. John R. Cowell needed time off to buy groceries and, you know, sleep.

But Big Edna failed to mention that she was fucking John R. Cowell, ex-bicycle repairman, and that their usual method of foreplay involved a case of Moosehead beer, a bag of Cheez Puffs, and thirty feet of rope. Big Edna described this scenario to me days later, during a combination heartfelt apology/plea not to sue her.

She installed the system on the eve of Carol's birthday. I managed to talk Carol into skipping work for a quick trip to New Orleans. I chartered a flight out of Little Rock, the plan being to wine and dine her all day Friday and to fly back Saturday night. Big Edna assured me that she could complete the job if she worked constantly and got paid a lot. I was skeptical, but I had to trust her.

Big Edna also neglected to tell me that she had subcontracted the electronic burglar alarm to her cousin, another ex-Marine—apparently the only type of company that Big Edna keeps—who owned his own electronics business. And Big Edna held out on me yet again, failing to reveal that he smoked enough pot every day to fry the brains of an entire brigade. So as Carol and I took overpriced carriage rides from Jackson Square, an ex-Marine was installing complicated wiring in Carol's house while smoking roughly two pounds of grass and laughing hysterically at a penis-shaped stain on his shoe. Meanwhile, Big Edna and John R. Cowell, ex-bicycle repairman, drank Moosehead and installed bars on the windows. Somehow, they managed not to break anything.

Not even Big Edna knew—at least not until the subsequent police investigation and her own heart-to-heart with a certain toked-up ex-Marine—that her electrician left one bare wire poking out of the keypad, a wire all but impossible to see in the dark. And of course Big Edna and John R. Cowell, ex-bicycle repairman, had little time for a formal inspection because they were drunk and horny. They had recently purchased a speculum, an IV drip, and four bags of saline, all of which they felt eager to try out. I would not inflict the particulars on the reader even if I knew them. Big Edna offered to tell me all about it after I got out of the hospital, but I declined and tried not to throw up.

The Three Stooges were long gone by the time Carol and I landed in Little Rock, our stomachs full of etouffe and our minds on what we had done on the plane, locked away in the restroom, door bolted, hands clamped over mouths to muffle our moans and whispers, living for the sheer joy of the moment, fearful that too much noise would remind us that no one could hear it anyway, thus ruining the illusion of daring and intimacy. A wonderful trip, and on the drive home Carol said

I hope I remembered to lock the door. Nothing scares me worse than the thought of some stranger in my house

and I smiled to myself, knowing that for once strangers really had been there, not to steal or rape or murder but to fortify, knowing that Carol would look past the intrusion and see the benefits, the safety of alarms and the satisfaction of going to bed only once a night. I said

I'm sure you did

and kept driving south, toward one bare wire poking out of a keypad.

We finally arrived, the trip taking forever because all the Hurricanes and mid-air champagne necessitated six bathroom trips, and even as we pulled into the drive Carol was crossing her legs and jiggling all over the seat, chanting

Hurry up hurry up hurry up.

Before I could get the car in park, Carol jumped out and ran, passenger door swinging open like the hem of someone's coat caught in a closed car door (I thought, unable to stop the simile before it ate itself and disappeared), hunched over and staggering, right arm reaching out for the doorknob that must have seemed impossibly far away, and all the while I was fumbling with the handle, calling

No. Wait a second, dammit

but she wasn't listening. She was already turning the knob, key fitting perfectly in the new slot just like Edna and I had discussed, not even noticing the new door and bars on the windows or else too desperate to care. I nearly hanged myself, leaping like a fool out of the car before shrugging out of the seat belt. And while I disengaged, Carol dashed in the house and right past the keypad she had never seen, its thirty second delay counting down as Carol dropped her pants and I stumbled in the door.

And at the exact moment that a part of me first registered the sound of Carol's urine hitting water, I reached out with the index finger of my right hand and punched in the first number of her brand new security code, 00000, chosen in a heady moment of literary allusion. Five zeroes to stop the alarm, the one digit whose pad rested beside the partially exposed live wire. I touched pad and wire simultaneously.

And in that moment, flesh on wire, I found myself connected to the world, plugged into the millennial body electric, every television and microwave and night light and personal desktop computer and a smell like burning hair, all in me in a bright flash of white blue, amplified and so overwhelming that it could only become darkness.

Thus ends my first-hand knowledge of what happened. The following is speculation:

Apparently my electrocution blew a fuse, because my plunge into darkness more or less coincided with a power failure, my body likely falling in a lump as Carol's piss trickled and dripped and finally stopped. And after that she must have wiped, looking at the dead globe on the ceiling, wondering what had happened and what had caused that thump she likely heard. Perhaps she pensively called

Mike?

as I lay unconscious and extra crispy on the floor of her newly-secure home. She must have stood up and made her way to the living room, one hand trailing along the wall and one splayed out in front of her, until she found me lying in a heap, burnt out like an old light bulb.

So ends the hypothetical. Other things I know, thanks to Big Edna. I know that Carol's opening the door and my subsequent failure to punch in the code caused an alarm to sound in the home of John R. Cowell, ex-bicycle repairman. It tore the quiet in half, burnt through his bedroom door, shattered his vodka-and-water reverie and the orgasm he was about to have all over Big Edna's face, shattered too her approaching climax, the thought of which shatters my own imagination.

And after hearing that cataclysmic alarm, John R. Cowell, ex-bicycle repairman, unceremoniously removed himself from Big Edna, threw on his clean pair of pants, and was gone, driving at dangerous speeds, determined to protect the client. Perhaps this attitude survived his days as a Marine and all the alcohol he could throw at it. He flew through two red lights, a few stop signs, one mailbox, and at least three trashcans, all sacrificed to his dedication. Apparently I had hired the right man.

This was the highly agitated state in which John R. Cowell, ex-bicycle repairman, skidded to a halt in Carol's yard and saw the front door standing open, the house dark. This was his state as he leapt from his Chevy and hit the ground running, oblivious to the dew darkening his shoes. This was his state as he crept up Carol's front steps and peered in cautiously. This was his state as he saw Carol, whom, you must remember, he had never seen before, as she leaned over my unconscious body. And this was his state as he tackled Carol and pulled out his Taser.

By Tuesday morning I was out of the hospital and had paid John R. Cowell's bond. I informed him that he could now add the title of Ex-Security Officer to his resume. Carol had not spoken to me. When I next saw her, she pulled into my drive, wearing black flats and a platinum-studded-with-diamonds ring. When I next heard her voice, she told me I had just paid for Saturday.

And this is the way it goes. I buy a present and get punched. I buy a security system and nearly fry myself. I hire a guard who assaults the woman he is paid to protect. I go out to rake leaves, to touch the earth, its grass, its weeds, its roots, only to wind up lying on my back, nose misshapen, upper lip a bright and crusty red, breath laboring in and out of my mouth in a fine white mist.

The leaves felt brittle in my hands. A twig jabbed the small of my back. Above me, clouds dotted the sky like cotton rubbed across rich velvet.

And underneath me, a sound overwhelmed it all. I felt it as it traveled down my spine and through my guts, a deep vibration like the thrum of hidden engines, and I knew that, whatever else I might be wrong about, my life's core truth was electric.

Just Because You're Paranoid

I hated that car before I even laid eyes on it. Hell, I hated it before it was even a car. At first, it was only the idea of a car, no physicality at all, no shape, no color. You couldn't gas it up if you tried, because it did not yet exist, at least not to me. Now, my girlfriend Carol, she's different. To her, the car was realer than real. Anything can take on that kind of importance, a thereness that glows around the edges. And for Carol, nothing stands out that brightly unless it can screw up my life under the pretense of convenience.

See, Carol wanted me to get a new car. The fact that I didn't want one made no difference at all.

She hated my old car because of our second date, when we got hammered and she let me take off her pants in the back seat, where she promptly got stabbed in the ass by a salad fork, the presence of which I could not explain. For most people, the fork would symbolize my culinary habits or my poor hygiene, but Carol always associated it with the car, a pain in her ass both literal and figurative. To me, my old car was like a friend with whom I had shared adventures, vacations, and a river of beer. To her, it was an enemy.

Okay, so the car was an Edsel. I admit it; for the most part, those cars sucked. But this Edsel had belonged to my father, and to my grand-father before him. It had survived three generations of Seymours, a reminder of my obligation to be humiliated in the grand tradition of my forebears. I was genetically encoded to drive that car, even if the trans-mission was dying and it leaked oil from Pinedale, Arkansas, to southern Missouri. And yes, I admit that the upholstery needed some work. But I thought the holes gave the seats a homey, lived-in look. And sure, I seldom cleaned the car. But I was hoping the fast-food wrappers and old newspapers on the floorboards would shift attention away from the bad transmission and the leaky engine and the spring up my passengers' asses. Besides, an Edsel is pretty much a rolling trashcan anyway, so why not use it in the way that nature intended?

Truth be told, I just plain liked my Edsel. I considered it a sputtering metaphor for my feelings about technology. I said as much to my best friend Dray, and he said

Mike, you can't have a metaphor and go around saying hey, look at this metaphor here. Then it ceases to be a metaphor and becomes a slogan

and I said

Oh, shut up

yet he was right. He usually is, the bastard.

But Carol didn't want to hear about my family tradition or my technophobia. She only cared about the spring and the leaks and her unnatural aversion to old clunkers. And so for weeks all I heard was

Mike, when are you going to sell that car?

or

Hey, I hear Robicheaux Chevrolet is marking down their extended cab pickups

or

Michael Seymour, either you sell that rusted piece of shit you call a car or I will never go anywhere with you again.

She asked me to sell my Edsel over and over and over, then pleaded, then demanded. So that last quote had the ring of finality, of ultimatums delivered, of threats too serious to veil in suggestions or strategically placed advertisements. I had to choose—either her or the car.

After thinking it over for a week or so, I spent two miserable days begging her to take me back. I had decided to embrace my love/hate relationship with modern technology in a different way—by hating to sell the old car I loved and by loving to hate the new car I'd have to buy. Of course, that was when I planned to pick the new car myself, before this so-far-theoretical new contraption became a metaphor for my love/hate relationship with Carol.

Ah, but the begging—that put me in a position of weakness, where negotiation was out of the question. You can only use sentences like

Baby, listen, I don't care about the car, I'll buy any kind you want, just please talk to me or at least come out of that bathroom

so many times before they bite you in the ass. Yes, by the time I finished begging I had agreed not only to sell my three-generations-old Edsel, not only to buy a new car, but to let Carol pick the car and all its features. She also wanted to negotiate the price, and by that time, well, why not? In fact, I saw no reason for me to go to the lot with her at all. I even told her so. She said

Now, wait a minute. You mean you don't even care what kind of car you get?

and I said

Well, of course I do. In fact, you might recall that I wanted to keep my Edsel. But what's the point if you're going to decide everything regardless of what I think?

and she said

You don't appreciate anything I do for you

as if all this were a favor she was doing me instead of a browbeating. I had to come up with some kind of clever retort, something cutting enough to remind her who was the boss but sensitive enough to allow for the possibility of getting laid in my lifetime. So I said

Okay, baby, you win. I'll go with you

and yes, I know I left out the cutting part. Call me a coward if you will. But I know which side my bread is buttered on.

So I went with her. I sat at a crummy cheap table, ate donuts and drank Dr. Pepper, pissed four times, took one long and surprisingly pleasant shit in a freshly scrubbed toilet, and read two six-month-old copies of *Entertainment Weekly*, and every time the salesman tried to point out some feature to me, I simply nodded in Carol's direction and shrugged. Once when she was haggling over the extra cost of power windows, I tapped her on the shoulder and whispered

Why are you fighting for that extra hundred bucks? I've got too much money as it is

and she replied

Michael, I will not let you get screwed just because you can afford to let it happen

and I said

Well, why not? It's my money, and I'm tired

and she said

It's a matter of principle

and I said

Oh, well, as long as it's a matter of principle, let's just stay here all day

31

and then I shut up and let her dicker, just because it made her happy. Don't tell me I'm insensitive.

By the time Carol got through with that salesman, I owned a brand-new sapphire SUV with power everything and a six-CD changer, a graphic equalizer and separate volume and climate controls for the back seat, all for fifteen hundred dollars off the sticker price. They even threw in tax, title, license, and a full tank of gas. As we say in the vernacular, Carol done good.

But the feature that screwed up my life in new and interesting ways was the satellite tracking system.

All this happened before the days of standard OnStar service; back then, a system like that was something special. Carol wanted to surprise me. I knew she had demanded custom features, but I had given up paying attention to what kind. When we picked up the car, the system had been installed in the dash, satellite tracking complete with digital monitor and guaranteed-to-connect-every-time hookup. I had always wanted one.

So why didn't I ever buy one? Well, for one thing it would have looked pretty stupid in my Edsel, like attaching a gas tank to a push broom. For another, deep down in the basement of my mind I always liked the rush of getting utterly lost, when no tree and no road look familiar and you have to navigate by the sun, forced to think, to say

Okay, we were heading south and it's three in the afternoon with the sun out there to our right, so if we just bear to the left we should hit the highway eventually

but not being very sure you're right.

The real reason, though, is that the damn things scared me. Oh, I wanted one, really I did, just like I wanted the CD changer and the climate control and the windshield wiper on the back window. I wanted it, but even more, I feared it. It knew too many things. It made the hair stand up on the back of my neck even as my balls were shriveling into peanuts. And now there it sat, mounted in the dash of my new car. Carol said

Surprise

and I said

Uhhhhmmmmm

and she said

What?

and even though I realized my mistake immediately, it was too late, gone, there still being no machine that can unsay your blunders. I said

32

I love it

and smiled, a part of me really happy and the rest trying desperately to fake it, but Carol said

Oh bullshit, you're overthinking again. Good God, it's just a

and I broke in

I know what it is. I'm just surprised. I really do love it

smiling bigger than ever, feeling like my face was stretching out past my shoulders, and I prayed she would let it go because with the tracking system staring at me like a lidless dead eye, I felt stressed enough. And happily for me she said

You damn well better.

I squeezed her knee and looked at the monitor, considering the possibilities. Then, as if reading my mind, Carol said

Let's take it for a spin down roads we don't know

as she locked her seatbelt, the matter already decided, my fate as predestined as a story with an outline.

I started the car and headed south, and we drove for three hours, around curves and up straightaways, going too fast, listening to CD after CD. We loaded them according to decade for sheer variety—Beatles and Led Zeppelin and early U2 and Nirvana and Ben Folds, or The Doors and Bad Company and Motley Crue and Metallica and Kid Rock, always rock and roll, always only five discs. Every time a song changed we would try to find another road. Soon we were hopelessly lost.

But of course owning a satellite tracking system makes hopelessly lost extinct, so I said

Well, are you ready to try this thing?

and, though I had known it was coming, my stomach contracted with a mixture of excitement and fear and the cold pizza I had eaten for breakfast when she said

Yeah, let's do it.

There we sat on the side of the road, SUV idling, Carol flipping a switch that would send the invisible connector leading to a satellite tied to a computer in a room I'd never see, where a technician would ascertain the location of Michael Seymour and his girlfriend, Carol.

And as the screen in my dash hummed into life, filling my car with light a pale and vegetable green, a list of options appeared on the touch screen. One read

Talk to a Representative

and before we could discuss our choices, Carol pressed it. I was about to complain, but then a voice said

Welcome to Track-U. Good evening, Mister Seymour

just like that, no question, not is this Mister Seymour or can I talk to Mister Seymour or can you please give me your client number. Just Hello Mister Seymour. I said

Who is this?

and the voice said

My name is Irv, Mister Seymour, and I'll be helping you out today. Do you require emergency assistance, or do you need a route map to a street address or landmark?

and I said

Well, we're lost.

There was something familiar about Irv, a pitch in his voice that I could have sworn I'd heard somewhere before, so I continued

And by the way, Irv, you sound familiar. Do I know you?

and he said

No, sir. I live in the Northwest, and I see here that you're in Louisiana.

Here Carol narrowed her eyes and stared at me, suspicious. She wondered where I was taking this. I said

Are you sure? Maybe I signed a book for you, or ran into you at a talk show

and Irv said

No sir, I seldom read books and I've never been to a talk show

so I said

Well, maybe it was

but Carol interrupted, snarling

Michael

through clinched teeth. I smiled at her, shrugged, and decided to drop it. Besides, Irv had said something that interested me. I said

Say, Irv, you know we're in Louisiana. Bet you can't tell me where we are exactly, though.

I could discern the faint clickaclack of fingers on keyboard, the Morsian language of database living. I could hear Irv breathing, his inhalation marked by a slight rattle in his chest, a surprisingly loud whistle in one nostril, possibly signs of a mending cold. I wondered if a machine could mimic human frailty, if gigabytes of memory were enough to encode the aftereffects of a virus in a human bloodstream. I realized I was sweating. My heart beat rapidly. Irv said

Looks like you're on Morehouse Parish road number four, approximately halfway between the town of Bastrop and the Arkansas border. Your position is north-northeast of Bastrop and south-southeast of Crossett, Arkansas. Which town do you want to head toward, or do you want directions to an address or a specific landmark?

All that driving and we had barely left the state. Carol stared at me, at the monitor in the dash, back at me, waiting. Irv whistled and snorted, also waiting. And I was waiting too, for what I wasn't exactly sure. Nothing recommended Crossett over Bastrop or vice versa. I could think of no landmarks worth mentioning, no addresses that I wanted to try. So in absence of any better ideas I said

Just use my home address

this being first the only thing I could think of and second a test to see if they knew where I lived. I was exhilarated, frightened, when Irv only clickaclacked and snortwhistled two or three times before saying

If you'll look at your monitor, the map should be appearing now.

Sure enough, the map faded in, bathing us in its greenish glow like night vision, Irv saying

Is it coming through all right?

We watched our patch of road materialize, our position marked by a red icon shaped like a car, Irv's route from our location to my house coalescing into a pale yellow zigzag, and there we were, pinned down and dissected. I said

So that yellow line is our route, and its terminus is my house

and Irv said

Yes sir

and I said

And can you see all these roads on your monitor, Irv?

and Irv said

Yes, sir.

I thought about that. Never to get lost, never to ask directions of any blank-eyed slack-jawed inbred gas station attendant, never to unfold a map that cannot by any law of physics or technological breakthrough be refolded again the same way. And the price? Only knowing that somewhere, in Seattle or Walla Walla or Portland, some wispy little schmuck named Irv would always be able to find me, no matter where I went. I felt storms brewing. Carol must have felt it too, because she said

Michael?

just before I threw the transmission into drive and said

All right Irv, let's see what you can really do.

I slammed down on the gas, sending a fan of gravel behind us, rocks careening off the undercarriage. I didn't care. I glanced back and forth from the road to the map. Carol shouted

Michael

but I ignored her, hearing Irv say

What are you doing, Mister Seymour?

calm as a dead pond, toneless as a machine. I saw a road to the right and cranked the wheel hard, our ass end sliding in the loose gravel, Carol shrieking as we headed toward the ditch before the back tires caught and we righted ourselves. The red car on the dashboard map dutifully turned down a new green path, only a second or so behind me, the yellow trail fading and realigning itself to reflect our new position. I said

I'm testing this thing, Irv old man. I'm seeing how good it is

and Carol said

Oh for Christ's sake Michael will you please slow down

and I said

If I'm going to have this thing in my car, I have to know how much they know and how fast they can access it

and Irv said

I'm right here, sir. Why not just ask me?

so I said

Oh, sure, you don't have any reason to lie to me, do you?

I saw another road, this one little more than a trail. I turned right again, hard, obliterating a road sign shot so full of .22 holes that no one could read it anyway, Carol now screaming

Michael

as the back tires scraped over a culvert, the headlights stabbing down what I was calling a road, grass growing down the middle of it, trees reaching toward each other like lovers linking hands over our heads. Dutifully, the red icon turned down a green road, the yellow ghost of our undriven path changing direction again. I growled

Dammit

and Irv said

We have that road in our database as well, sir. What are you trying to prove here?

That was a good question. What was I trying to prove? That I could outrun the sound of Irv's voice? That I could drive past the gaze of satellites I'd never see and men I'd never meet? In truth, I had no idea. All I knew, and all I know, is that sometimes you just have to drive really fast. It's the only thing that makes sense.

Up ahead the road was ending. A metal gate stretched in front of us; beyond it I could see bales of hay pockmarking some farmer's meadow. Irv said

Your road is ending, Mister Seymour. I suggest you turn back. And let me assure you

but I interrupted

Don't assure me, Irv. The only person I really trust other than my agent is sitting beside me

and Carol said

That's sweet and all, Michael, but if you crash through that gate in this new vehicle I will personally fucking castrate you.

But I couldn't listen to her, not then. I had to know. I had to see what Irv could see, what his computers could discover by connecting the right one to the right zero. I pressed the gas harder, gripped the wheel at ten and two. We hit the gate at a speed approaching sixty miles per hour. Its high-pitched scream battered our ears as it bounced to the left, trailing sparks behind it like satellites. And then our front tires flew over the uneven ground, the wheel jerking out of my hand, my body rising off the seat, the lap belt yanking me down again. Carol was shouting at me, the words lost in the whirling chaos I had created.

I tried to grab the wheel again, but we hit a hole and I banged my head on it instead. And as we flew through the meadow, I glanced at the dash. The red icon was still there, but now it moved through blackness, green paths falling steadily away. I knew then that I could find roads that Irv could never see. And as we headed inevitably toward a looming haystack, Carol beat me about the head and shoulders, her blows staccato like fingers on a keyboard, and Irv's voice, disconnected and calm, said

You know, you could have just turned the system off.

Doesn't Mean They Aren't Out to Get You

As usual, it started with something benign and quickly built toward catastrophe. I needed a new cookbook, but I couldn't stomach the thought of standing in the paperback aisle at Wal-Mart. Every time I go there, one of two things happens. Either somebody recognizes me and snatches one of my own books off the shelves, wanting an autograph—an action Wal-Mart managers frown on unless the fan has already paid—or everyone mills around me, trying to watch without looking like they're watching, waiting to see what I'll buy. Then they all grab the same book, as if I've got the inside track on what's fine literature and what isn't. Don't they know that some authors have bad taste? I mean, have they seen the crap that some of us publish?

But I really needed that cookbook. I mean really. My culinary repertoire consists of grilling whatever I can buy or run over. I'm also a talented baker of fish sticks, corn dogs, and crinkle-cut French fries. Other than that, I'm lost.

My girlfriend Carol isn't much better. She can throw together a hamburger casserole, and she once made a bean salad that almost didn't put me in the hospital. But neither of us is entirely sure what a pinch of salt really means, or whether a pinch is more than a dash, a peck, a sprinkle. Neither of us is sure how to broil without charring or why anyone would cook with a bay leaf if you can't eat the goddam thing. Why not just throw in a chunk of quartz?

No, Wal-Mart works fine when I need groceries or a television or a gas-powered grill. But it would be too much hassle to bother with for a lousy cookbook.

Ah, but wait, you may say. Why not just go to a different store? Well, for starters, there is no other decent retail store in Parkview, or anywhere closer than Pine Bluff or Monroe. And who wants to make a two-hour round trip just to pick up a book? What about small bookstores, you say? Well, the mom-and-pop places around here don't carry cookbooks, at least none that I've ever seen. They're all about the literary—Faulkner, Proust, Woolf, Hemingway, and some contemporary writers like Digby Darrymore. I can buy my own books there, but I can't buy a decent cookbook. So I have to choose between two evils—Wal-Mart's increasingly anorexic paperback section and the subsequent mob scene, or the long drive.

Monroe or Pine Bluff or Little Rock present similar problems; I don't get recognized as often as, say, a movie star, but at least a few people always manage to spot me, and then it's Wal-Mart all over again. The last time I went to a bookstore in Pine Bluff, I had the wonderful luck of walking in just as the clerks were building a ten-foot front wall display of my newest novel, symmetrical stacks piled up like miser's coins, and over the shelves a poster-sized picture of my face, the one from my first book's dust jacket, four years old and a bit thinner about the cheekbones but still recognizable. The clerks spotted me, looked at the picture, looked back at me, back at the picture. I put my index finger to my lips and hissed

Shhhhhhhhh

but one of them shouted

Holy jumping fuck on toast, it's Michael Seymour

which is a sentence I'd love to use in a story. Totally ridiculous, but with the right character, it could sound laugh-out-loud funny. The problem is that no one would ever believe a real live person had actually said it. It sounds too much like fiction-writer dialogue. I almost wish I had made it up, because when that clerk shouted it, my day was shot. Everyone turned and stared, and then I got bombarded by teenagers and middle-aged librarian types and one woman so ancient she looked positively mummified. I spent over two hours autographing hardcovers. The manager even tried to pay me for my impromptu appearance, but I just wanted out of there.

Now don't get me wrong. I don't mind signing autographs by the dozens when I'm on tour. And I'm fine with autographing the odd book or two when I'm recognized. I mean, you take care of the people who take care of you, right? But when I've planned a day full of errands and maybe a lunch with my girlfriend, don't expect me to smile when you pen me up for two hours. Writers have to eat, too.

Now you're probably thinking that Carol could just buy the books for me, but I've got you there, too. Remember how small towns work? In Pinedale, Parkview, Crossett, Monticello, and thousands of other cozy little hamlets, everybody knows everything about everybody else. If your hound dog is humping your next-door neighbor's prize-winning poodle behind the gardenias, you and your neighbor may hear about it after the mailman, the meter reader, everyone who lives on your block, and everyone they've ever met. In a town like Parkview, information is like an airborne germ, passing from mouth to mouth on the wind.

My point? Everyone in Parkview knows that Carol and I are dating. And apparently the rule stating that all authors have fine and insightful literary taste applies to authors' girlfriends, too. Whenever Carol stops in Wal-Mart's book section, the same crowd nonchalantly gathers around her, with the same results. She's even been asked to sign a few autographs. All the attention annoys her, so she won't buy me any books, even if I say pretty please.

Anyway, I was trying to solve my cookbook conundrum when my best friend Dray knocked on my door. He didn't wait for me to answer, in fact rarely does; once he knocked and walked right on in, catching Carol and me in an erotic but difficult-to-achieve position, both of us staring wordlessly at him as he burst into laughter and backed out of the door. This time, Carol was working at her office over in Pinedale, and I was both fully clothed and unaroused, thank God. Seeing Dray inspired me, so I said

Drayton old buddy old pal old chum

and he closed the door, shook his head, and said

Oh no. Whatever it is, forget it. The last time you called me old buddy old pal old chum I got stuck on a blind date with a toothless 78-year-old widow

and I said

You'd rather have dated a 78-year-old with teeth? You should have said so. Besides, this time all I need is a cookbook

but Dray's eyes widened and he shook his head even harder, saying

Oh no, I'm not going near a book section anywhere in Arkansas, Louisiana, Mississippi, or east Texas. The last time I bought a book for you, I was chased out of a Target by sixteen women who wanted me to explain the subtextual misogyny in your characters. When I told them all I know is that your mother didn't breastfeed you, one of them threw a flower pot at me and accused me of going Hollywood

and I said

41

Well, did you?

and Dray said

I don't even know what going Hollywood means. Besides, I never buy retail anymore

to which I replied

Hell, no. You can't blame me for that. It isn't my fault if everybody follows you around the goddam Gap.

Dray burst into laughter, a certified guffaw, the kind that causes one to double over, hands on knees, eyes squinted as if in pain, the kind of laugh that eats itself into a squeaky near-silence. Personally, I didn't see what was so damn funny. I said

Well, I'm glad you're having such a jolly time, but I need that cookbook, damn you

and Dray wheezed

I'm sorry, man

so I said

What's so funny, anyway?

and he said

Two things. One, the notion that I would ever enter a Gap, even under threat of torture. Two, your colossal ego. Do you really think that people follow me around for insight into your fashion sense? Earth to Mikey: everybody values your literary taste. But even Carol doesn't think much of how you dress.

To this I immediately thought of a dozen nasty retorts, but in all honesty Dray was probably right. He usually is, the bastard. In any case, arguing with him was getting me no closer to owning a cookbook. Trying to keep him talking while I figured out a new angle, I said

Well then, why don't you go to retail shops?

and he said

Because retail stores, much like government offices, seem intent on recruiting the laziest and most unfriendly, incompetent, ignorant, surly, depressing people imaginable.

I couldn't argue with that. Nevertheless, I simply could not allow Dray to leave without helping me. The very concept of frozen dinners made my stomach churn and gurgle, and I was sick of the same old meals. And so it happened innocently. I was only trying to keep Dray busy without allowing him to dash my plans to bits, and so I asked

Well, then, how do you buy all your stuff?

Dray laughed at me again. He shook his head, as if he were amazed at such a childish question. He said

If you would ever get your head out of the books in your head, you might have heard of a little thing called the Internet.

Heard? Ha. I had more than heard of it. I had taken blatant advantage of it. I owned the michaelseymour.com domain name. I also owned mikeseymourrules.com and killseymour.org, two sites that mainly consisted of message boards dedicated to, respectively, the praise of and vehement criticism toward everything I write. I, of course, write some of my own reviews, both the glowing ones and those that read like a bipolar first grader's stream-of-consciousness rambling. Once, I even engaged in a war of words with my own agent. Poor Darlene never knew that she was defending me from myself.

I had also explored the Internet's omnipresent chat rooms, finding them a far better and cheaper version of the therapy sessions I used to attend, where I would pluck out all the barbs and nettles from my soul and pay two hundred dollars an hour to a goateed man who stared out the window and mumbled the occasional mmm hmmm. I used the Internet to find movie showtimes in Monroe and Pine Bluff. And, like every other person on the planet, I used it to forward jokes to everyone I knew.

I had not, however, actually bought anything through my computer. I have always been afraid to provide personal information, including my address and credit card number. I worried about identity theft, not to mention the possibility of a psychotic fan's stumbling upon my address and showing up on my doorstep armed with a machete and an autograph book. Still, I could hardly allow Dray's insult to go unanswered, so I said

You buy everything online? Damn, son, and you call me paranoid

and he said

No, no, it's nothing like that Sandra Bullock movie you're probably playing in your head, the one with identity theft, and I'm not agoraphobic. I do it because I can sit in my living room, naked and unshaven, and buy anything I want without meeting even one God-this-job-sucks-and-I-hate-customers sales clerk.

I had to admit that his idea had merit. I don't worry too much about unfriendly sales clerks; if I had to spend my days making change behind a cash register, I might be surly too. But anything that increases my opportunity to remain naked and/or unshaven seems worth investigating. So I said

But I don't even know how Internet shopping works

and Dray rolled his eyes and said

Well, let's log on and I'll give you the fifty-cent tour.

Thus began my foray into the world of online consumerism. I had a cable modem; much faster than using phone lines, it was the best kind of connection to have back then. So all we had to do was double click on my Internet browser icon and my home page, michaelseymour.com, appeared on screen. Dray sat down in my comfortable leather chair, forcing me to squat beside him like a little kid at his father's desk, the bastard. He clicked into the browser's search window, deleted my homepage URL, and typed in www.bigfuckindeals.com. He said

This is my favorite shopping site. You can get damn near anything for decent prices, and traffic is lighter because the name turns off your average housewife.

I nodded seriously and said

Mmmm-hmmmm

and he said

Now check this out.

He clicked the GO button and my computer, utilizing its superfast processor and the wonders of digital cable, immediately loaded the most dangerous page I have ever seen. The homepage of bigfuckindeals.com was well-organized, symmetrical, a three-column job. The right third of the page trumpeted customer-controlled features—wish lists, email notifications, that sort of thing. The middle section advertised what was allegedly the Big Fuckin Deal of the Day. On this occasion, the holy grail of bargains was Digby Darrymore's first novel *Toejam Falls*, a wildly popular book in spite of some of the worst reviews I have ever read; *Entertainment Weekly* called it a sad waste of potentially useful toilet paper. I almost laughed out loud and wondered if Digby knew his beloved first book had been discounted 70% off and was receiving an average grade of C- from bigfuckindeals' obviously astute and tasteful customers.

But the left side—oh my God, the left side promised so much.

The heading read

STORES

and under it, such a list. DVD, Music, Video—which, I assumed, meant VHS, still relatively popular back then—Computers and Video Games, Home and Garden, Outdoor Life. Links to every kind of product that man or woman could possibly want. Here one could order a

44

theater-quality hot-air popcorn machine and the popcorn itself and a home video system and the movies and theater chairs.

I know this because, on that very day, I ordered a theater-quality hot-air popcorn machine and the popcorn itself and a DVD home video system and the movies and the chairs, thereby maxing out my Visa and earning approximately five zillion bonus points on bigfuckindeals' customer reward program, said points immediately cashed in for more movies. Hey, you never know when you might need an extra copy of *Ace Ventura II: When Nature Calls*. Dray watched all this with a species of horrified fascination, making comments such as

Sweet jumping Christ, Mike, what the hell do you need with fourteen theater seats? You don't even have room for six in this house

or

Oh, yeah, Mike, great choice. I've always wanted to know somebody who owns every Ed Wood film ever made

but hey, Ed Wood had charm if not talent, so I didn't really give a crap what Dray said. On that same day I also purchased a new outdoor gas grill, a digital camcorder for my computer, and a stereo system, all using my American Express. By this time Dray was sorry that he ever showed me the site, sorry that he had ever forced me to get a computer and an Internet connection, sorry that he had trusted me to act like an adult. But what's the use of having more money than you know how to spend if you don't enjoy yourself once in a while? If I couldn't fit fourteen theater seats in my living room, I could always get a bigger house.

Dray, the bastard, pointed out that I didn't even have fourteen friends who would come over at the same time. I said

Yeah, but you never know when I might want to host a literary cocktail party. I could have a salon like Gertrude Stein's in Paris, invite Digby Darrymore over and use copies of his shitty novels for kindling just to get under his skin

and Dray said

Mike, you hate cocktail parties. Come to think of it, you hate people. Why don't you just admit that you just want to look at all this stuff every day and congratulate yourself on your own success?

and then he stormed out, slamming the door behind him. That might have hurt my feelings but for one small detail—he was right. He usually is, the bastard.

But should I apologize for being successful? Should I live in a two-room shack in the woods and drink muddy water from a polluted spring just so nobody will think I'm a snob? Should I give back my new SUV with all the trimmings, just because somebody else can't afford one? Should I feel guilty just because I'm better off than some people?

I guess the answer to all those questions is yes, because I felt damn guilty. Dray makes good money and owns a nice place over on Cottonwood —two stories, manicured lawn with those hideous gnomes popping out everywhere like weeds, some kind of family four-door wagon even though Dray's single and probably always will be. Still, he has to save, budget, make sure whatever he buys won't keep him from eating for a month. Compared to my spending power, he's in strictly You Want Fries With That? territory. So spending half his yearly salary on stuff I didn't really need was not the most sensitive thing I could have done.

I resolved then and there to make it up to him in the only way I could think of—buying him something on bigfuckindeals.com.

So I searched. I looked for DVDs, but I couldn't remember if Dray was a Hitchcock man or a Kubrick aficionado or a Roger Corman junkie. I thought about buying him a home theater system, but I had no idea what was compatible with Dray's set. I considered one of those new scooters, the kind that run on batteries and respond to your body movements, but I thought of how silly beanpole Dray would look rolling down the street on that thing and couldn't stop laughing long enough to make the search.

So in the end I bought him a bigfuckindeals.com gift certificate in the amount of five hundred dollars. He never said thank you or even told me what he bought with the damn thing, but I sure felt better. The problem for me was that I couldn't stop once I got started. I had found a new addiction—typing in a few numbers, clicking a couple of computer buttons, and having stuff magically appear at my house.

I never went to bed that night, sacrificing sleep to the gods of bigfuckindeals.com. I bought Carol a new set of dishes, a peach duvet and a matching set of sheets, a subscription to the *New Yorker*, and fifteen CDs. I bought my agent a new coat for those chilly New York evenings and a copy of Digby's first book, though that one was a gag gift. I bought my editor a copy of a do-it-yourself book-editing kit, another joke, and four or five Matisse prints. I bought my great aunt a foot massager. I collapsed on the couch at dawn, eyes bloodshot, back aching, bank account several thousand dollars lighter. I felt elated and woozy, like I had just smoked a pound of really good grass. I slept most of the day and woke up happy.

But around seven or seven-thirty that night, that bastard Dray showed up, and he wasn't alone. He knew what I'd been up to, knew it because he knew me, knew that I had bought too much and had probably done so in vain, since in my entire gift-buying history, people have liked my presents maybe four times, and that's counting the Valentine I gave Mindy McDonald in third grade. Because he was right, as usual, Dray's presence would have been bad enough. But he brought Carol. He brought my great aunt Millicent. He brought my agent Darlene and her husband Morrie, my editor, and how he got them to drop everything and hop a plane from New York on just a few hours' notice—hell, how they'd managed to find a flight in the first place—was a mystery that I have yet to solve. They all filed into my living room, solemn, funereal. No one even said hello; they just walked in and surrounded me, herding me out of the living room toward the patio, where comfy lawn furniture and hundreds of mosquitoes were waiting. I knew what was happening; I had been through interventions before. I decided to head them off, saying

Look, I know why you're here, and you're too late. I've already bought a bunch of stuff and logged off and I've been sleeping for hours, haven't even checked my email since late last night, so there's really no need

and Dray interrupted

Shut up, Mike

and Carol said

Michael Seymour, I can tell by your baggy, bloodshot eyes that you've done it again. What the hell is wrong with you?

and I said

What do you mean, what's wrong with me? I have money and I spent some on myself. Then I spent some on all of you. What's the problem?

and Carol said

The problem is that I called your accountants this morning and they reported a one-night credit card activity of almost nine thousand dollars

and I said

Now wait a minute—how do they know that already if I just did it last night? Who's watching me?

and Darlene said

Mike, you can't make this about your paranoid fantasies. We know you've got money, but you won't have it for long if this keeps up. And we all know that it will keep up until we stop it for you.

They were closing in, cutting off all escape routes—Dray in front of the doors, Morrie behind me, Darlene and Carol to either side. They were inching closer, slowly, ready to pounce. It was like *Night of the Living Dead*. I said

Now wait just one fucking goddam minute. I'm a grown man and I can spend my money any way I please. You all just back up and let me be. I don't need an

and then they all fell on me, Morrie behind me on his hands and knees in the old schoolyard position, Dray stiff-arming me backward ass over elbows, Aunt Millicent and Darlene and Carol jumping on my arms, Morrie rolling over and sitting on my legs. I grumbled

Goddammit, get off me. I'm old enough to be President of the United States. I've written two best-sellers and an award-winning short story collection. You can't just sit on me and take away my stuff. I'm not a fucking kid. Get off.

But nobody got off, and Dray, the bastard, ambled into my house, unhooked my computer, and brought the hard drive outside. He stopped near the doors, too far away for me to reach even if I could have used my arms. I had given up fighting by then anyway. Even if I wanted to hurt those people, which I didn't, they had me pinned, and I was too out of shape to push them off. I was trapped. Dray raised the hard drive high over his head and said

We love you, Mikey

and brought it down on the concrete. The computer smashed apart, the casing flying over my head, CD-DVD/RW drive bouncing off Morrie's chest as he sat on my legs. I shrieked, kicked, flailed, but only for a moment. I knew it was too late. My computer was dead, smashed, sacrificed on the altar of my mental health and financial security. Morrie said

I think that's sufficient

and got off my legs. Aunt Millicent and Darlene and Carol released my arms and backed away from me. I sat up and glared at Dray, snarling

Well, I hope you're happy. You come to save my finances and you smash a machine that cost me three thousand dollars

and Dray said

I'm going to buy you a replacement. Call it my penance for starting this whole mess. And I'm going to have a security function installed, the kind that parents sometimes have to use for their juvenile delinquents. It won't let you visit any retail or pay sites. Carol will check with your

48

accountant every two days, just in case. If you go on another crazy buying spree, we'll be back for the new computer, too. And after that, you'll have to peck out your books on a broken-down Underwood. I shit you not.

With that, he walked back through my patio doors. I heard him making himself a drink at my bar, as if he owned the place. Carol hugged me and said

He's right, Michael. You just don't have any self-control

and I said

I know he's right. He always is, the bastard. But that doesn't mean I like being sat on

and Darlene said

Sorry about that, Mike. By the way, we want to see fifty new pages by the end of next week. You've dawdled long enough

and Morrie said

We have to catch our flight in three hours, so we've got to be on the road. Come to New York in a month or so and we'll have lunch, hash out some plans for revision. OK, Mike?

and I said

Whatever

and Carol said

Don't sulk, Michael.

That's the way things go around here more often than not. They all treat me like a child—me, the best-selling, award-winning, present-buying, forty-something author. I buy them presents, using money I earned, money that's languishing in my accounts, and they literally sit on me and smash my computer. I can never figure out if they do it because they like to control me or because I really need that much maintenance. I'll have to ask somebody in my chat rooms; they'll probably know.

The only good part of that whole incident, though, is that I never got to buy that cookbook. So Carol had to eat franks and beans and corn dogs until she could get around to ordering one herself. The look on her face as she swallowed yet another Oscar Meyer nearly made up for my own humiliation. And at least somebody else had to do the work for a change.

I Know This Guy, See?

I know you've heard stories that start off this way: I know this guy, see? You know, like the girl who swears she really really really has a cousin who went to school with somebody whose ex-fiancée once slept with a dude whose sister-in-law knew a chick who passed out at a party and woke up in a tub full of ice and a note saying I've taken your kidney, call 911 if you want to live. Most of these stories are pure crap—maybe the kind you have to study for a while before you flush, but crap all the same.

I've got one, too; I'm not too proud to admit it. But I didn't hear it from a guy who heard it from a guy who heard it from a guy. I didn't hear it from my girlfriend Carol, who demonstrates little patience with myths, urban legends, tall tales, and true stories that sound made up. I didn't hear it at work around the water cooler. This is not a joke, nor a joke disguised as a story. It's all true.

I know this guy—let's call him John Smith—who had made a nice life for himself. He wasn't in Bill Gates's league, but he was doing okay. He lived in southeast Arkansas, which doesn't exactly have a high cost of living, so he could afford a Range Rover, a Trans Am, a two-story house on River Road complete with Spanish moss hanging on all his cypress and oak trees, a below-ground heated pool and a guy to clean it. He mowed his own lawn on a machine that looked like a tractor on steroids. He gave money to charity. He was doing well.

But he was lonely. Now, I don't mean he was alone. A successful person is never alone. There's always somebody willing to ride your coat-tails, to take your money and your food and your liquor and your cum. John could get blown whenever he wanted and could stick his dick in a fine selection of southeast Arkansas poontang on any night of the week. He could even cuddle if he wanted to. And yet he still felt lonely. He told me once that holding somebody who was more interested in your stocks than your opinions was like kissing your sister. It might work when you're drunk, but you're ashamed of yourself in the morning. All the gold-diggers made him gun-shy; he didn't want to commit to anybody until he felt certain that they weren't just after his bank account. His problem, you see, was paranoia. When you get the notion that everyone's out to get you, you can't just conveniently put it away. John wanted someone he could trust but saw everyone as a potential threat. He didn't know what to do—until one day when he was strolling through Wal-Mart and found the answer to his prayers. Unfortunately, he also sounded the death-knell of life as he had known it.

He was browsing through the electronics department when he spotted it—a computer program set amidst games like *The Sims* and anti-virus software. It was called *Virtual Mate*; the subtitle read *If You Can't Make It in the Real World, Go Virtual.* John picked it up and studied the box. On the front cover, a cartoon man and woman stood next to each other, smiling; cartoon lightning bolts arose from their joined hands, symbolizing perhaps the electricity of their touch. Or maybe the picture was meant to be literal, because the woman's legs were made of ones and zeroes, which were connected to a cartoon computer monitor by more lightning bolts.

John turned the box over and read the following product description.

Tired of the old dating game? Then try ours. No more searching for the perfect mate; no more wasting tons of money on flowers, candy, dinners, and movies; no more wondering if you'll get a good night kiss, or even more (wink, wink). With *Virtual Mate*, you get all the conveniences of dating—companionship, conversation, intimacy—and none of the aggravation. And if you are really, really brave, you might even try our Virtual Marriage feature, brand-new to this, our latest version. Ready to take the ride of your life? Install *Virtual Mate*, register on our site using the Automatic Registration feature, and wait for your first Virtual Connection. Then pick the girl or guy you want, and *voila.* Your dreams can all come true. [For Mature Audiences Only]

John was intrigued. So he checked the system requirements, bought himself a copy of the software, and headed home.

At least he enjoyed a decent dinner before he committed financial suicide. He took himself out to eat at the local Western Sizzlin'—not exactly Tavern on the Green, I know, but in southeast Arkansas, you take what you can get. It was Saturday night, the evening of the Sizzlin's all-you-can-eat seafood buffet, and though John hated the burnt stuffed crab and the slimy corn fritters, he loved fried fish and shrimp. He ate for two hours, and when he finally left fifteen percent on the table and stumbled out the door, his stomach felt bloated, as if he had consumed roughly half of the marine life on earth, all washed down with glass after glass of sweet tea. He drove the five miles from the Sizzlin' to his house, a trip fraught with small-town stoplights and speed traps, desperately craving three things: a long piss, an even longer shit, and a few hours at his computer with *Virtual Mate*.

John, you see, was not a religious man in the strict sense; you might call him a foxhole convert, always calling on the Lord when he needed something and putting God away in his junk drawer when life seemed fine. He never attended church services, so he could sleep late on Sunday after a long night of caressing a pixelated tit. As he sat on the pot, farting out tiny chunks of half-digested shellfish, he read a two-year-old copy of *Atlantic Monthly*, focusing on a short story by the for-some-reason-critically-lauded Digby Darrymore. Digby's an acquaintance of mine whose redundancy is matched only by his pretensions. John once told me that reading Digby's prose was the lingual equivalent of receiving a barium enema; the end result might be good for you, but the process itself really sucks. I have no idea why he chose Digby's long, apocalyptic tale "The Bridegroom's Bride" for his crapper reading—perhaps only because it would last throughout his equally apocalyptic dump.

Later, John mixed himself a Jack and Coke and sat down at his desk. He popped open the CD drive and dropped in the *Virtual Mate* disc, little realizing that he would later be able to chart his ruin from the instant he pressed the Close button and the disc began to run. The start menu looked dull, the usual combination of graphics and Hey This Is the Best Software Ever advertisements. Clicking past them as fast as he could manage, he found himself staring at the registration screen. You're generally given a choice: (a) register your product immediately over the Internet (FAST, EASY, AND YOU'LL HAVE FULL ACCESS TO OUR HELP LINE AND SOFTWARE UPDATES), (b) register your product by snailmail (Just Fill Out the Handy Card), or (c) register later (and the software always seems to be going for the guilt trip here, sort of like your mother does when you decline to ask your younger brother along on your hot date). But John was given no such choice. *Virtual Mate*'s online registration form listed only two possibilities. One button said

Register

and the other read

Cancel

a set of instructions whose implications could hardly be missed: you either tell us what we want to know, or you might as well eject that disc and hang it from your rear-view mirror.

These two possibilities failed to alarm John. He did, however, dislike some of the questions, especially knowing that he had to register online, and God only knew how secure the server would be. They solicited the usual claptrap: name, address, how many computers in the house, how many games a month you buy, and so forth. But this one also asked some rather personal questions that should have sent a paranoid guy running for the hills. John was pleasantly drunk, though, having already made his way through three Jack and Cokes. So he answered questions about his social security number, his bank routing codes, his net worth, the kinds of investments he had made, even the makes and models of any boats, automobiles, or ATVs he might own; he also answered them truthfully. I'm sure he got about half of it wrong, working from a pickled brain, but he got enough of it right to start all the trouble.

At this point, I could make a cryptic announcement, like

Therewith he endeth his life

or state a moral, like

Never give out important information to people you can't sue

but I won't, because the point here isn't to teach you a lesson or tell you a story with a beginning, a middle, and an end. All I can tell you—all that's known, because John drank so much that he blacked out and lost a big chunk of the evening—is that he apparently used the software to create his Virtual Mate.

He saw her for the first time when he restarted the program sometime the following day. Her stats indicated that she was 5'10", though of course on-screen she was only 11" or so, a true Barbie girl. She had salmon-colored hair, like you only see on computer-game-generated women or punk rockers. Her breasts were enormous; perfectly round, they stretched from her neckline to her navel, a gravity-defying feat even in virtual reality. She sported a pinched nose, thin like a dime, and full, pouty

54

lips. Her blue eyes nearly pierced the screen. But what really disturbed John were her eyebrows—or, rather, her unibrow. Spanning nearly the entire width of her face, this thing looked like someone had sewn a wool scarf on her forehead. Whole armies could have lain in ambush inside it. Once, over beers at my house, John said

I swear, Mike, she looked like what would happen if Pete Sampras and Wendy Whoppers had a kid.

I don't even like to think about that image.

John couldn't imagine what he had been thinking when he created this Frankenstein Mate. But since he wasn't actually required to sleep with her, looks weren't the real problem. In his fucked-up state, he had apparently thought it funny to create a character that merged all the personality attributes of a raging lush and a slut. He named her Muldoon, of all things, and her profile read thusly:

Muldoon Smith is a 21-year-old aspiring model [John, like many of us in our 30s and 40s, fantasized about the pleasures of younger women]. She exercises four hours a day to keep in shape and spends time shopping her portfolio and attending auditions. She is not much of a housekeeper or cook. Muldoon drinks too much; she never met a whiskey sour she didn't like. Also, the pressure to stay thin has contributed to her anorexia. Muldoon loves hot sex but will only sleep with well-hung men; we're talking double digits. She enjoys foreign films and Three Stooges shorts. Her pet peeves are selfishness and people who talk about subjects other than herself.

John read that profile—one that he had created with the help of his lovely new software—with horror. He didn't know what was worse—that he had created a self-involved anorexic alcoholic nympho or that his drunken self had apparently thought such a creature might be fun. Sober, he was not so amused. For one thing, John loved party girls like he loved spicy Mexican food—fun to eat, but ultimately, they give you too much shit. For another, John discovered that he had sent *Virtual Mate* his own penis size, which, at five inches, fell far short of the range his new mate required. Therefore, he was immediately worried that Muldoon would refuse to sleep with him. He had no desire to be rejected by women who did not even exist. Perhaps even worse, John knew Muldoon's type; he had dated a couple of anorexic models in the past, finding them far too high-maintenance for his taste. He worried that his creating a mate so similar to those women indicated a fascination with the type, a need to buy himself trouble. But he was mostly concerned with his new software. He had bought it for fun, but he had used it to create a harridan.

Still, just for the hell of it, he decided to try Muldoon on for size. So he turned on the program.

The screen faded in slowly on a rotating ceiling fan. Virtual John was obviously waking up, the computer simulating his first-person point of view. The camera panned to his right; the other side of the bed lay empty. In the background stood an open door, through which John could see Muldoon kneeling in front of a toilet. The sounds of vomiting filled the room, the computer providing a helpful caption:

Huuurrrrrkkkkkgggghhhhh-UH-hurrrrrrrrrkkkkkggghhh-UH.

Hung over in real life, John nearly puked. But he managed to keep last night's dinner in place long enough to notice a series of choices on screen. How should he handle this delicate situation? His options—rather limited, he thought—were to ignore her, to call out and ask if she needed help, or to go in the bathroom and check on her. He decided to be sensitive and choose the latter. So his virtual self swung out of bed and walked to the bathroom.

Muldoon continued to retch, and Real John's stomach continued to flip-flop. He wanted to turn down the volume, but he had paid for the program, and by God, he was going to get his money's worth. He stared at the screen as his character approached Muldoon, who paid him no mind. His virtual hand reached out and touched her shoulder, his virtual voice asking

Honey, are you OK?

Real John smiled, thinking that his virtual self was, so far, proving to be an ideal husband. Apparently Muldoon didn't agree. She jerked away from Virtual John and turned toward the screen, barking

Get away from me, you asshole. How dare you even touch me, after you let me make such a fool of myself last night? And on our wedding day.

Real John jerked backward as if she might reach through the screen and hit him. He was flabbergasted. How dare this skinny pixilated bitch shout at him that way? But then, he thought, that's actually a fairly typical response from that kind of woman; they always wanted to blame someone else for their problems. He had experienced enough mornings-after to know how the situation should be handled. New choices appeared on screen: apologize and leave the room, shout at her, or slap her. Now, John had never been a violent man in real life. Once he kicked a cat that had bitten him after he accidentally stepped on its tail, but he had never raised a hand in anger in his life, especially not to another person. But Muldoon was only a simulation; no one could really get hurt. And he had bought the software to try a new dating experience, right? So he decided to see what would happen if he chose the slap option. As soon as he clicked his mouse, his virtual arm shot out and backhanded Muldoon, who fell over the toilet and banged her head on the bathtub. Green puke dribbled from the corner of her mouth. Virtual John shouted

Don't you talk to me like that

while Real John recoiled, shocked at the sound of flesh on flesh and bone on ceramics. Like the barfing, it all sounded too real.

Muldoon lay on the bathroom floor for a moment. Then she grabbed the toilet bowl and pulled herself up to a sitting position. She looked pathetic. The sounds having unnerved him, Real John actually felt bad about resorting to virtual violence, and so when a new set of choices revealed that he could help her up, he chose to do so. His virtual hand reached out again; Muldoon flinched. Now Real John felt even worse. But then she reached out and took his hand. Virtual John pulled her upright; she picked up a hand towel and wiped her mouth. Then she turned to Virtual John and said

Honey?

And then she kicked him in his virtual balls.

Virtual John fell to the bathroom floor, writhing in pain. Real John cried out

Holy shit.

The sounds of vomiting again poured from the speakers, and Real John knew that Virtual John was puking this time. Onscreen, Muldoon leaned over Virtual John, her face filling the screen. She said

If you ever hit me again, you son of a bitch, I'll have you arrested. And you can forget about getting any pussy tonight, either.

Then the screen faded to black and a pop-up menu appeared, asking Real John if he wished to continue or quit. He chose the latter; he had had enough of those realistic retching noises, the sharp crack of open hand on flesh. He shut down his computer, showered, and fell asleep on the couch, already exhausted from living with a woman who didn't really exist.

He slept for four hours and awoke feeling refreshed. He was hungry, so he drove back to the Sizzlin' and treated himself to a New York Strip and a baked potato, with plenty more sweet tea. He left feeling better than ever, returning approximately six hours after shutting down his computer. When he opened the door, he did not at first notice the faint glow from his office. He sat on his couch and watched the news, and then he flipped channels for a half-hour or so, not really seeing any of the programs, the hangover fading until it was a ghost in the back of his mind. But eventually he needed to check his email, so he got up and headed for the office. And when he saw the glow, his stomach flip-flopped again, the positive feelings evaporating like dew on a hot day. The room should have been dark, the monitor dead, blank. But somehow it had turned itself back on.

He walked around his desk and sat down in his chair. He looked at the screen. Muldoon's face stared back at him. She was smirking.

John was dumbfounded. He had no idea why the computer had restarted, nor how *Virtual Mate* had turned itself on. All he knew was that he wanted out of the program; just looking at the glowing screen, the smirking face of the virtual harpy he had created, made him shiver, the chill crawling up his spine like a spindly bug. So he grabbed his mouse. But as soon as he touched it, Muldoon scowled and said

So there you are. Who do you think you are, running out on me the day after our wedding? You think you can just slap me and then leave?

Real John literally jumped out of his chair and cried out. Muldoon's unibrow was knitted in rage; it looked as if she had grown a Groucho Marx mustache on her forehead. John tore his gaze away from it and looked at his options, wanting to be cautious until he could figure out what was happening. So he clicked the Grovel button. Virtual John said

I'm sorry, honey, but I had some things to take care of. I didn't mean to worry you

but Muldoon said

I wasn't worried, you jerk. I'm mad as hell. You get me drunk and let me dance naked on a table, in front of all my friends, and the next morning you slap me and then just leave? What kind of a husband are you?

Her face screwed itself up into something resembling a bulldog sucking a lemon as the game paused and waited for Real John's response. And at this point, he was good and peeved. Her voice sounded deep and throaty, like Harvey Fierstein, and she was saying all the right things, playing on his guilt for slapping a woman, even a fake one. In other words, Muldoon was punching his buttons as effectively as any real person ever had. Feeling defensive, he instructed Virtual John to fight back. So Virtual John said

Well if you weren't such a psycho, I might have stuck around. Or have you forgotten how you kicked me in the balls? And how is your dancing on the table like a slut supposed to be my fault?

and Muldoon said

You weren't as drunk as I was. You could have stopped me

and Virtual John, with no prompting from Real John, said

Yeah, sure. You were too drunk to stop yourself, but you were sober enough to turn me down last night. I bet I'm the only new husband in the world with a raging case of the blue balls

and Muldoon said

What did you want me to do, barf on your cock? Not that that pathetic little piece of shit deserves anything else

and Virtual John said

Yeah, well, you've never complained before. And is that liquor I smell on your breath? Are you drunk again, you goddam lush?

and Muldoon spat

I have to drink to keep from killing myself. You've already made me miserable. And I'll tell you a secret: I've never complained about your shitty screwing before because I've been getting it from Mike Seymour on the side.

Now imagine Real John's surprise when my name came up, especially in that context. Of course, the alleged affair between me and Muldoon had never happened, since, you know, Muldoon didn't exist. Plus, I don't date chicks with unibrows. My girlfriend, Carol, keeps her brows plucked into thin curved lines like the accent marks over foreign words. But that's neither here nor there. What's important is that Real John hated being compared unfavorably to another guy, especially in terms of his sexual equipment. The fact that his critic didn't really exist made no difference to him; he was hopping mad. So he looked at his choices and clicked

Bitchslap her.

Virtual John's hand shot out and crashed into Muldoon's cheek. Her head rocked back like she had been shot. She stumbled backward and fell over a couch (one that, Real John insists, he would never have bought in a million years). She moaned.

Now Real John's choices read

Go check on her

Tell her she got what she deserved

Kick her while she's down

and while the game paused again, his nastier impulses shouted to choose the last one. And he felt sorely tempted. He wanted to watch that animated foot plant itself in her shimmering midsection, wanted to hear what kind of oomph noise she would make. But as he deliberated, he felt himself calming down again and knew that he shouldn't give in to those kinds of urges anymore, even in a game. So he clicked on the first option. Virtual John scrambled around the tipped-over couch and cradled Muldoon's head in his virtual hands. She moaned again, her unibrow knitted in pain. Real John noticed for the first time that she had a gold tooth. Of course she did. He shuddered as Virtual John said

Oh God, baby, I'm so sorry. Are you all right?

Muldoon pushed Virtual John away and sat up. She rubbed her jaw and then checked the back of her head, likely looking for virtual knots or blood. Real John noticed that she was not crying. The imprint of Virtual John's hand looked cartoonishly red on her face, like Hawthorne's birthmark blown up two hundred times. Now Real John was presented with several dialogue choices. He chose

I didn't want to do that, but you just drive me crazy. Why would you say something like that to me?

Muldoon stood up; Virtual John did the same. Real John expected another kick in the balls, but what happened seemed much worse. Muldoon approached the screen, her unibrow almost brushing what would have been Virtual John's nose. She planted a little peck on the screen, presumably on virtual lips. Then she said

I said it because it's true, Tiny. And you just slapped me for the last time.

With that, Muldoon turned and walked out the virtual door. The scene faded to black, on which the following words appeared in red, the same red as the handprint on Muldoon's cheek:

Your Virtual Mate has left you. Divorce proceedings will begin immediately.

And then the computer shut itself down.

Real John had gotten caught up in the freedoms of creating a cyber-persona, a self that could do things he would never do. And he couldn't pretend that none of it mattered, that he could somehow wipe away his morals and ethics in the name of playing a game. He was disgusted with himself, but he was really pissed off at the manufacturers of *Virtual Mate*. They had brought him to this low point. He had no idea how the software could shut down and start up his computer at will, but for now he wanted no more online love; he wanted what so many men want when a romance, even a fake one, goes bad: a cold beer and a ball game. He grabbed his car keys and drove toward Pine Bluff, where, a little over an hour later, he pulled into Stoney's, his favorite sports bar, and tried to forget about the way his virtual handprint had looked on Muldoon's already-frightening face.

The first scent of real trouble came when he tried to pay for his beers with his VISA. He handed the card over automatically, not even taking his eyes off the game. Even when the waiter returned, he barely acknowledged the man's presence. He assumed, as any of us would, that the waiter was simply returning his card and the check for him to sign. But the waiter did not lay the rectangular pad back on the table and wish him a good day. Instead, he said

Mr. Smith, your card was declined. Would you like me to try again?

John looked up at the waiter as if he had just announced that Martians had landed on the roof and were knocking back Jell-O shots while impregnating brunettes with the power of their minds. John enjoyed immaculate credit, earned with a lifetime of purchases and carefully rationed installments, with promotions and new tax brackets. He could not be over the credit limit; he had at least a thousand dollars left. His account could not have been frozen because he made his payments early and always sent in more than the required minimum, an annoyance to the card companies to be sure, but hardly a reason to close an account without notice. He shook his head, blinked several times, and said

What?

so the waiter repeated

Your card, Mr. Smith. It's been declined. It says your account has been closed and that I'm to cut up your card

but the waiter didn't tear it up. He handed it back to John and shrugged, as if he knew how it felt, the humiliation of having your personal life suddenly made public by the appearance of scissors and the infernal clicking sound they made when snipping through hard plastic. John was still confused, unsure of what he should do or say, so the waiter eventually said

Perhaps I should try another card?

but John said

No thanks, I'll just pay cash.

He took out two twenties and handed them to the waiter, telling him to keep the change, a generous whim he might not have indulged had he known what was about to happen. But at the moment he only knew that his VISA had been declined, something that had never happened to him before, even by mistake. John left the bar shaking his head and mumbling to himself about the likely sexual inadequacies of VISA employees. He drove to his bank and pulled up at the drive-thru ATM, intending to get more cash; if his VISA had gone wonky, he could just use his other credit cards, but he wanted some ready cash just in case.

He pushed his card into the slot and punched in his PIN number (1234, he told me later; after all, why try to hide it after all that had happened?), selecting the withdraw option. But before he could choose from his checking and savings accounts, the ATM shut him down. Across the screen came this message, and with it John finally realized just how much his life had changed since that morning:

Your card has been confiscated due to insufficient funds. Please contact our offices during regular hours.

John said

What?

but the ATM did not reply. He snarled

What the fuck do you mean, insufficient funds? I've got at least four thousand dollars in that goddam account.

So he tried punching in the numbers again, but the machine did not respond, did not change its message or spit out his cash, so John did what anybody would do in such a situation. He slammed his hand down on the whole keypad, hard enough to sting, and shrieked

I do not have insufficient funds, you piece of shit

but of course the machine remained silent, its green unblinking message staring at John as he became angrier and angrier, and also nervous, his VISA and his debit card both dead in one night. He had broken out in a sweat; he felt a pulse beating in the middle of his forehead, where a vein always popped up when he felt particularly stressed. His rational mind told him that something had gone very wrong, but rationality was fast slipping away underneath a wave of frustration, beer, and bright red fright. He began ranting, punching all the buttons on the keypad in no particular order, swearing at the ATM, its manufacturers, the workers who had installed it and their spouses and kids and pets and chat room pals, the bank itself and all its officers including the ones who had helped him procure the loans for his house and cars, the U.S. mints in Denver and Philadelphia, the Treasury Department, the federal government, and whoever came up with capitalism in the first place. He claims he even swore at Marx and Engels for failing to create an alternate system that actually works, but I'm a bit dubious on that point. In any case, he went totally batshit.

And so, of course, before long someone drove by and noticed him hanging halfway out of his parked and still-running car, assaulting an ATM, screaming at the top of his lungs that he wanted his card back and he wanted it right fucking now. Soon the police came, and their flashing reds and blues attracted a crowd of rubberneckers, many of whom knew John, the rest of whom began calling for his immediate conviction because they believed he had been trying to rob the bank like a socially retarded, good-for-nothing parasite. John swore at these people, at the cops who arrested him, at the department that hired them, at the mayor, even though he had no idea who the mayor of Pine Bluff might have been. He was getting around to cursing the name of his state senator when the cops finally managed to shove him into the patrol car and roar off, John's car still idling at the ATM while a few stragglers wondered if they should move it, leave it, or steal it and sell it.

John used his phone call to contact his lawyer, a luminary with the rather questionable name of Allred C. Berggdorff. Personally, I wouldn't hire a dog walker named Allred C. Berggdorff, but John trusted this guy, had used him before, even kept him on retainer. Berggdorff was a general litigator, meaning that he dabbled in everything and specialized in nothing; John thought Berggdorff would be perfect for his current troubles, since it seemed to involve everything and stem from nothing. The first thing that Berggdorff said was

If you're broke, how do you plan to pay me?

and John snapped

I'm not broke, you asshole. I couldn't possibly be broke. Just get me out of here.

So as soon as John had been arraigned, Berggdorff paid the bond and drove John home, where John found that his key no longer worked. He rattled the doorknob in disbelief, then kicked the heavy oak door and nearly broke his right foot before Berggdorff managed to reach around him and pluck away the paper that had been tacked near the bell. John was shouting something like

and when I find out who meddled with my locks I want you to sue them till they bleed, those bastards

but Berggdorff wasn't listening. He was reading the paper, which turned out to be a court order banning John from the premises pending his divorce proceedings. It further notified John that all his assets—bank accounts, credit cards, bearer bonds, the stock he owned in Microsoft and Apple (he was always a man who hedged his bets, except when buying stupid computer games)—had been frozen. Berggdorff recognized the name of the judge who had signed the order, so there was no doubt as to the document's veracity.

John sat down on his front steps, his head spinning with confusion and anger. How could divorce proceedings possibly be pending when he wasn't really married? How could his assets have been frozen in response to a lawsuit filed by a woman who did not exist? And how had it all happened so fast? He leapt up and ripped the order out of Berggdorff's hands, scanning it quickly. He wadded it up and thrust it at Berggdorff, saying

This has to be fake, even if it's got a real judge's name on it. It has to be. How could Muldoon hire a lawyer in the first place? She's a fucking computer-generated image. She can't just walk out the front door and drive to some law office and demand a divorce

and Berggdorff rubbed his chin thoughtfully, nodding, and said

I'm telling you that this document is legit. I've seen Judge Thatcher's signature enough times to know it. But you make a good point. If your wife isn't real and couldn't hire a lawyer

as John broke in

She can't have a real case.

Berggdorff clapped John on the back and said

Look, this is the American legal system we're talking about. I'm sure that somewhere there's a precedent for something like this. Let me do some digging and get back to you tomorrow afternoon. In the meantime, we don't want to violate this order. Do you have a place to stay?

John had a place to stay, all right—my place. He showed up at my house in the middle of the night, looking haggard and wild-eyed. He banged on the door until I staggered out, naked as the day I was born and pissed off, having been in the midst of a fine erotic moment involving my girlfriend Carol, a pint of whiskey, a curling iron, and a dozen donuts. Carol seemed equally annoyed until she saw John, looking all disheveled and needy. Then she agreed to let John stay at my place indefinitely, even managing to fix him up with several of my outfits, a toothbrush, his own razor, and the most comfy spare bed in the house, all before I had time to process the concept that John had managed to automate domestic disturbances.

Not that I wouldn't have let him stay—he's my friend. I never complained about his living with me, even though it lasted for over eighteen months, during the nastiest and most disturbing divorce I have ever seen or heard of. The first thing John wanted to do was check the *Virtual Mate* website, to determine whether he had missed any caveats or fine prints or flashing neon warning signs. So we fired up my PC and Carol opened my Internet browser (I was no longer allowed to go online without supervision, the result of an online shopping spree that got a bit out of hand). John shooed her out of the way and typed in the site address. He spent the next ten minutes clicking on every link he could find, and just when he had almost decided to give up, he found the following notice, buried deep in the FAQ section between advice on file sharing and a disclaimer regarding changes in product specifications:

Virtual Mate is designed to replicate every part of the marital process. As such, you should be very very careful when constructing your Mate. Your software will provide you with several documents and ask you to agree to *Virtual Mate*'s terms. You must fill out all documents completely and accept the terms of use. For your own sake, read each document carefully before accepting.

John read this notice over and over again, for so long that Carol and I began to glance at each other, worried, thinking that perhaps he had blown a crucial synapse. When we tapped him on the shoulder or called his name, he ignored us. He was mouthing the words as he read, though he said nothing aloud. Finally he turned, slowly, my leather chair creaking underneath him, and when he looked at me, I almost screamed. His face had turned completely white, eyes wide and utterly hopeless. I had seen that expression before, and always on the news—victims of fire, flood, and hurricane. Children staggering away from a burning village. Middle-Eastern residents plodding through rubble-strewn streets in front of a bombed and smoking building. But I had never seen it in person and never over a woman, certainly never over a game. And having seen it, I now understand what it means when we say that someone is lost. Carol said

John? What is it?

and he said

I was really drunk when I created Muldoon. I don't remember any documents. No documents at all.

The next day, John got up long before us. He called Berggdorff first thing, who begged John to stop bugging him and let him work. John would comply for about twenty minutes, and then he would remember something that Berggdorff needed to know or some question that needed to be asked. He paced and pulled his hair and smacked a fist into his open palm and cursed Muldoon and his own stupidity.

Berggdorff didn't come around until almost seven o'clock that night. He looked exhausted, almost as haggard as John. When I let Berggdorff in, John ran up and embraced him, then shook his hand so hard and long that I was afraid Berggdorff's teeth were going to fall out on my carpet. I had to pull John away as Carol gently said

Let's let him give us some good news before we kill him with gratitude, okay?

and John nodded, still trying to thank Berggdorff and shake his hand at the same time. I think John still believed that everything would be fine, that Berggdorff had managed to make it all go away, had revealed the suit for a ridiculous and money-grubbing stunt. Even then he had hope. All that changed when Berggdorff sat down on my couch and said

Look, John, this isn't the end of the world.

There's another expression that I had never understood before: his face fell. John educated me on that point, too. All the muscles holding his face together simultaneously drooped—mouth, eyes, cheeks, even his nose, as if his head were melting like a popsicle on a hot July day. He ceased his manic leaping about and padded over to my recliner, the one that faced the couch. He sat down and arranged himself—feet together, knees touching, spine straight, hands folded and placed neatly in his lap. Once he was settled, he closed his eyes for a moment, as if in supplication. Then he said

All right, Allred. What's not the end of the world?

Berggdorff laid out the case in detail. Apparently in his drunken haze, John had in fact agreed to the *Virtual Mate* terms of service, which constituted John's consent to contract with Virtual Mate Incorporated as his equal domestic partner. In other words, he had married the company. His Virtual Mate Muldoon Smith was named as the company's representative. In the event of the contract's dissolution, represented through a Virtual Divorce, half of his assets would default to Muldoon, and therefore to the company. As soon as John accepted the terms, Virtual Mate Incorporated's lawyers drew up the proper paperwork and filed it during the next business day. Thus, while John's so-called marriage was not legally binding, his arrangement with the corporation was. Hearing all of this, John said

But I didn't sign anything. Can they do all of this without my signature?

and Berggdorff said

I'm afraid so. Litigation that affects a person without his or her permission happens all the time—wage garnishments, actual divorce proceedings, et cetera et cetera. Even if that weren't true, though, the *Virtual Mate* terms of service specifically state that checking the acceptance box shall constitute a legally binding signature and that the signee thereby waives all rights to contest the terms of a Virtual Divorce. I read it myself. Don't you remember that part?

and John said

I don't remember any of it

and Carol said

Mr. Berggdorff, this is insane. How can they get away with this? I mean, this is Arkansas, not California. Our divorce laws don't automatically divide a couple's assets equally; they have to hammer the details out themselves, or let the lawyers do it

and I asked

Now wait a minute. Why do you know that?

but she ignored me, instead listening as Berggdorff replied

It's all in the language of the contract. Again, divorce laws don't apply. Business laws do, and no law says that a plaintiff has to be a living, breathing human being or that a plaintiff's representative has to be a live person.

Now if that doesn't prove that the world's just one big nuthouse, I don't know what will.

So began John's long stay in my house, during which he cried for two solid weeks, moped for months, and threw one of my chairs out a second-story window for no apparent reason. During that time, Carol managed to spend thousands of dollars on him—new clothes, food, the whole nine yards. Of course, the thousands of dollars were mine, not hers, but she spent them anyway. I even paid his legal fees. Berggdorff kept reminding us that somebody had to pay him, and the first thing we established was just who that somebody would be—me.

I guess if you're looking for a lesson here, I could say *caveat emptor*. But that seems kind of silly. After all, John lost half of his possessions to a company because he drunkenly married a virtual woman—not exactly a situation that applies to most people's lives. In fact, I think all this raises a lot more questions than it answers. I mean, I've never married anyone, virtual or otherwise, and yet my assets are also under someone else's control; I can barely use my own bank card to buy a damn donut without Carol's express written permission. At least John had a court order telling him how and why somebody else was running his life. But as for the rest of us, sitting across from our wives or boyfriends and negotiating every little thing like it was the goddam Versailles treaty—how did we get ourselves into this? I wish I knew a guy who would tell me that story.

It's All in the Reflexes

Paris saw it in Wal-Mart on August fifth, the anniversary of his first love's leaving him for a horn section band geek. Probably a trombone player, since those guys are used to pumping hard, though I think Paris would probably tell you it's because they're used to blowing with all their might. He's bitter that way. He has similar prejudices against Jewish computer programmers, WASPy business executives, and high school quarterbacks. Curiously, he has no such disdain for the closeted lesbian he dated. When she left him for another woman, he wasn't upset. He simply said that he would have liked to watch. But I digress.

I want to tell you about the time Paris bought himself a video game system and thereby almost ruined both our lives forever. See, I have these issues with technology. Every time a new gadget changes my pattern of existence, my paranoia flies out of control. It all goes back to a bad child- hood experience with a baby monitor, or maybe it was my wind-up swing and how my mother left me in it for hours at a time, sometimes neglecting to rewind it so that I would hang suspended in what looked like an oversized diaper attached to metal rods, picking my nose and crying, wondering even at that tender age if my Mom hated me. When I tell that story, people accuse me of exaggerating or simply inventing it all, claiming that no one could remember something that happened so long ago. I say bullshit. I do remember that swing, and I have taken a solemn vow never to buy one if Carol and I ever have kids. But there I go again, trying to tell a different story, one about me. Carol says I do that too often as it is. So back to Paris and his Makazaki Playbox 9000, the latest in video game technology.

All this happened a few years back, before your video game system would also play Blu-Rays and surf the Web and make hot buttered popcorn. Of course, I wouldn't really know what they can do, since Carol won't let me buy a new one. She controls all my purchases; I'm basically a kept man. The last thing I bought was a steak at a fancy New York restaurant. I was treating my editor and agent to lunch. They had driven in from the Hamptons and were hankering for some Chilean Sea Bass, a fancy-schmancy dish that all rich people are supposed to eat. Me, I don't like it, so I ordered a Porterhouse, the thickest one they had. I also ate a baked potato and a house salad, and I drank too much beer, which led to what has become known as The Neiman Marcus Incident. But that too is beside the point, which is that I don't really know much about today's game tech. Carol says my writing should keep me far too busy to worry about kid stuff anyway, and who knows; maybe she's right. But then, she also says that I'm too self-involved, that it's a miracle I manage to tell stories about other people at all, so what does she know? Here I am, telling a story about—who was it?

Oh right, Paris—he was a video game nut. The kind of guy who had mastered *Asteroids* and *Donkey Kong* before you had played your first game of pinball in a convenience store or movie theater lobby. The jackass who played *Frogger* for seven straight hours, miraculously managing to hear all the ooohs and ahhhs of the easily impressed while ignoring all the boos and hisses of those who wanted a turn. He owned all the high scores on *Defender* over at Wal-Mart and could play *Q-Bert* and *Dig Dug* simultaneously. This guy wasn't just fascinated with machines; he was a machine.

Naturally, he also owned an Atari 2600 when we were kids. He bought *Adventure* before anybody in town (think poor man's *Legend of Zelda*, if you've never heard of it) and *Yar's Revenge* and even all those games you had to play with the godforsaken paddles. We spent half our childhoods inside his bedroom, slamming our joysticks and thumbing the old red button, and for perhaps the first time ever in the history of storytelling, neither of those images is euphemistic. We broke his plain old black-with-single-red-button joysticks within a year, so his Mom bought him two fancy new ones for his birthday, the kind that looked like the trigger mechanism on a fighter plane—buttons galore in exciting new places, a bigger stick, more torque for your hard-driving gamer. Given those *double entendres*, I guess gaming really is the new masturbation.

Anyway, the Atari went out of style in the mid-80s, and while we could have gone with an Intellivision, things just weren't the same until

Nintendo came along. Soon Paris owned a Super Nintendo, and then a Nintendo 64, and Sony's Playstation, and then Playstation 2, and Xbox from Microsoft, and the Nintendo Gamecube. I won't even mention the Sega systems because, well really, why bother? Nobody bought them.

I'd advise you to ask Paris about the Playstation 3 and the Xbox 360 and the Wii, except that Paris's shrinks won't let him game anymore; they're afraid he'll reawaken his psychosis. And hell, even I had enough sense not to go as far as he did. I have to admit, though, that I sometimes wonder what it would be like if Paris and I could play again.

We can't, though. Even if Carol would let me buy a new system, even if the courts would let Paris game once in a while, his doctors have become the leading voices in denouncing video game violence. Really, I can't blame them. Paris had his whole life in front of him—a cliché, I know, but true nonetheless. He was still in his early thirties when he bought the Makazaki Playbox 9000. Even then, he seemed odd—a yuppie who lived in Little Rock, not New York or Los Angeles. He was making the big bucks, easily six figures, which goes a lot farther in Arkansas than in Chicago or San Diego. He had a fiancée named Anne; she came from a well-to-do family with ties to the conservative Republicans who had opposed Clinton's first presidential run. Paris hailed from that lower-middle-class segment of the population that Republican quote tax breaks unquote tend to ignore—in other words, the people who really need them. But Paris had made good through hard work, dedication, and a well-timed trip to the john at an office party, in which he had found his boss on top of an intern from marketing, a strapping young man with, Paris said, a huge stiffie of his own and the boss's cock in his mouth. Two days later Paris had been promoted to Vice President-Sales. In fact, that promotion was largely responsible for his decision to buy the Playbox. He wanted to celebrate. An innocent decision, yes, but one with unforeseen consequences for both of us.

One morning I had just finished my early writing session, having produced around fifteen hundred words, a good day's work on average. I felt even more welling up in my mind like water bubbling to the surface of an underground spring, and I could tell that, if only my stiffening back held out, I could get maybe fifteen pages of good, solid text by the evening. I said to myself

Mike, you will not let anything distract you. You will eat your lunch, take your afternoon constitutional, nap for an hour, and then get cracking, and you will not stop until you finish that scene where the cat launches its attack on the spaceship

and so naturally that's when my phone rang, the annoying sounds of Yankee Doodle Dandy dribbling through the house like a gas leak. I'll never let Carol choose my ring-tone again. I thought of dumping the call to voicemail, but I made the fatal mistake of checking the number first. The readout said

Paris Woolsley

so I answered it. You've got to keep in touch with your friends, as my best buddy Dray always says. And he's right as usual, the bastard. I said

Paris, my man. I was just thinking about you.

Okay, so I lied. But you might as well make people feel good when you can. It's like telling someone how great they look when you cannot, in fact, see anything different about them at all. We all do it. Anyway, Paris was really bubbling on the other end of the line. I could see him in my mind's eye (a cliché I have never understood and would never, under any circumstances, use in a story), cavorting around his living room as he said

Hey, Mike. I've got some ultra-freakin'-cool news

perhaps looking like he really had to pee or had just gotten bee-stung on the ass. I giggled a bit, hoping I wouldn't have to explain, as I was trying to focus all my energies on the book. I shouldn't have worried; I don't think he even heard me. He went right on with his half of the conversation, saying

I just bought a Playbox 9000 and five new games. Get your ridiculously white ass on over here and let's break this sumbitch in.

I took exception to this comment, because my ass isn't that white. Sure, it's hardly ever seen the sun, but I don't think that makes it any whiter than most white people's asses. I once saw a plumber's ass—well, half of it, anyway, the crack grinning at me like Kilroy as he bent over my upstairs bedroom's toilet—and it looked way whiter than mine. Plus, Paris knew that I write once in the morning and once in the afternoon. He also knew that I had been hoping to buy a Playbox myself, and that I would therefore find his offer irresistible. My good friend Paris had ruined an excellent, productive day for me by offering me hours of fun. I couldn't really be mad at him, but I wished that he had bought the damn thing on Sunday, the one day of the week that I don't write.

But call he did, and go I did; I left as soon as I hung up. He lived in Little Rock, so I had a two-hourish drive ahead of me. I navigated the bumpy and tedious roadways of southeast to central Arkansas, the sameness scrolling by like background scenery in a *Flintstones* cartoon. I got stuck behind an elderly couple who pulled out in front of me, causing me to slam on my brakes and nearly drive my SUV up their ass end. Of course they then proceeded to drive 32 miles per hour, which made me want to park the car, walk up beside them, and slash their tires. I cycled through two CDs between Monticello and Star City, a distance generally covered with only half an album or so. And the whole time, I sat boiling in my seat, white-knuckling the wheel, full of Paris envy. Paris had no Carol to castigate and/or castrate him, so he was actually in a much better position to buy fun but ultimately useless machines. Not that I regretted her presence in my life—I love Carol and would not, under any circumstances, trade her for a Playbox 9000. Well, I might be tempted if someone assured me that the Playbox would never deny me sex if I forgot to call my mother on her birthday. But no matter how happy I felt in my own life, I couldn't help but envy Paris's freedom. I had to have a taste every now and then, a little vicarious living between friends.

So I decided that I was going to have a blast at Paris's place and would refuse to acknowledge my jealousy, any residual anger at Carol, or any possibility that Paris was cooler than me. I would simply show up, play the game, and then leave, betraying nothing. This plan worked, at least until I actually walked into Paris's apartment and saw that he had started without me. Then I said

You asshole, you said you'd wait for me. And is that *Underworld Quest XIX* you're playing?

He grinned, knowing what *UQ* meant to me. I had followed the franchise through its first eighteen incarnations and had beaten each one, no matter how long it took or what it cost. In fact, I had lost three early girlfriends to the game. One broke up with me after I had been playing *UQ V* for three straight days. This marathon occurred at Paris's house, so I blamed him. He didn't mind, since he never liked the girl anyway. The second breakup occurred as soon as I bought *UQ VII*, since this woman was a friend of the first video game casualty. She actually presented an ultimatum as I was purchasing it, saying

Look, Michael, it's either me or the game. Choose

so I handed the cashier my VISA and never saw her again. After that, I managed to avoid losing any more chicks to video games until I bought *UQ XVIII*, what was supposed to be the last and greatest installment, the one wherein you could choose from fifteen playable characters, each with unique powers and skills, and a storyline that changed every time you made a decision. That game actually freaked me out, its intelligence and adaptability far too advanced for my tastes. Oh, it was fun and all, but I don't like games that can outthink me. They remind me too much of *War Games*, that old movie where a chess-playing computer nearly starts a nuclear war. Still, I finished the game, though not before another woman had packed up her spare toothbrush and panties, moving out quicker than I could lose my extra lives. I swore off the *UQ* games after that. So naturally, they released another iteration, one that focused on multiplayer interaction. Yes, you could use the Playbox's built-in modem to fight alongside countless and faceless other fans, this long before PC games started the trend and the consoles followed suit. *UQ XIX* was the first and, in my opinion, the best.

Back to the story—Paris had been playing for an hour and a half. He had chosen to be Grimlich, the Vampire Soldier, a mild-mannered Vietnam vet with equal parts tooth, knife, and bazooka. Paris had already racked up five thousand coins and had cleared two checkpoints. At one of these points, he had killed a werewolf character operated by a man in Idaho.

I plopped down next to Paris and said

Are we good to go?

and he said

Plenty of food and drink in the kitchen and my cell's turned off

and I said

Good. When can I play?

Paris didn't answer the question for three hours, during which time he killed four more characters, gathered a few thousand more coins, and pissed off the other players by destroying all the enemy monsters himself. Finally he lay the controller down and said

My hands hurt. Your turn.

Those words sealed my doom.

The game took a while to get used to; I admit that. I'm not a natural like Paris, not at adventure-type games, anyway. I spent thirty minutes creating my character, who was immediately eaten by a hungry sphinx guarding the entrance to a pay toilet in a post-apocalyptic city. I therefore had to spend the next hour creating a new character, choosing my abilities much more carefully. I named this one Rodric the Retrograde and actually killed the sphinx this time. The pay toilet turned out to be a portal to a complex sewer system in which I encountered a plethora of venomous slugs, a couple of super spiders, and one very hacked-off vampire. Another player was controlling the vampire, and I saw how Paris had known the werewolf was from Idaho. A little readout beside the vampire read

Fred Jones, Atlanta, GA

for about three seconds, before I scrambled up a nearby ladder and opened a manhole, inadvertently flooding the passage with sunlight and turning Fred Jones's vampire to dust. Fred cursed in ways I had never heard before. I assume those words are indigenous to Atlanta. He even managed to call me a few names before the game booted him out, as if it were my fault he had chosen to play as a vampire.

Next, I navigated through a series of underground tunnels, and yes, I know, putting a manhole in an underground tunnel isn't logical, but I didn't design the game. I wandered around for half an hour, looking for treasure or a monster to kill or another playable character to disintegrate, but I found nothing. I mean nothing at all. I could see only darkness, a big black screen. I began to wonder if I had uncovered a programming bug or a joke that the creators had slipped in. Bored, I said

What the hell is this shit?

until Paris wandered into the room, holding the house phone to one ear as he ordered a few pizzas, and said

Oh, I've been through that. Just keep going forward and you'll come out of it soon enough

so I did. And sure enough, the screen soon began to fade in on a cavern, from which more tunnels branched off. As the image coalesced, I saw a hot chick standing near one of them. Okay, sure, she was a video game chick, nothing more than a series of binary digits, a set of pixels on Paris's TV screen. But what a set—I mean, you had to admire her creator's sense of design. She had slender legs and huge boobs, like a comic book superheroine. Her long blonde hair was braided and curled over one shoulder. Her outfit tied together down the front, affording glimpses of boob and washboard stomach; her thigh-high boots had laces that wound around her hips. She looked like Wonder Woman crossed with Lara Croft crossed with Xena, Warrior Princess. Had she been a real woman, I would have asked her out and dealt with Carol later. Since she wasn't real, I simply had my character make contact with her and then, speaking into my headset's mouthpiece, said

What's a nice girl like you doing in a cave like this?

I was never going to meet the real woman, so I didn't have to come up with a great line, okay?

Anyway, she didn't immediately incinerate or disembowel me, so I took that as a good sign. She said

That's cute. Your voice sounds familiar ... have we played together before?

and though her voice did indeed remind me of someone's, I said

No, I don't think so. This is my first time. I killed a vampire in the sewers and made my way here through the tunnels

and she said

Yeah. These tunnels get confusing if you've never been here before. Where are you headed?

and, having no real idea, I said

I don't really know. Where are you headed?

and she said

I'm gathering energy points so I can go into the Forbidden Swamp and kill the Giant Strangler Toad. If I can do it, I get to skip three experience levels and warp straight to the Paradise Inn. Want to come along?

I had nothing better to do, and Paris was taking a shit, so I said

Sure.

She introduced herself as Cynthia Markovich, though her character's readout had already told me this. I also read that she was from Luckenbach, Texas, the town from that old Waylon Jennings song. I didn't even know it was a real place. Apparently, Cynthia was not much of a reader. Though I had foolishly put in my real name when creating the character, she didn't ask me if I were that Michael Seymour or whether I might be willing to autograph a book through the mail. Or maybe she just hates my stuff. In any case, we chatted for a bit as our characters made their way out of the tunnels, my Rodric the Retrograde following her Athena the Asskicking Amazon, since she seemed to know the way. As we talked, I learned that she was a manicurist and that I should watch out for carnivorous earthworms, as they tended to pop out and gobble up your health points.

By the time we reached the swamp, Paris had finished his business and was once again sitting by my side. Perhaps not realizing that the player on the other end could hear him, he said

So. Who's the bimbo?

I winced. Cynthia, who had been telling me all about her sister the hairdresser and her disgusting, unemployed brother-in-law, suddenly went silent. Simultaneously, Athena stopped walking along the swamp path. Not good. I wanted to continue the game, and hanging out with Cynthia/Athena seemed a good way to jump a few levels. That would make Paris really jealous, an added bonus. But since I didn't actually know Cynthia, I wasn't sure how to handle this problem. So I said

Uh, that wasn't me

which was lame, I admit, but the only thing I could think of. Cynthia said

So who was it?

and I said

My buddy Paris. He's a moron

while making never-you-mind-you-got-me-into-this motions in his direction. Paris giggled like an adolescent. I was actually starting to miss Dray's pretensions and lectures. Cynthia said

Tell Paris he's a sexist pig

and I said

I agree

and she said

Then why hang out with him? I don't think I like you anymore.

I was about to ask her how she could so quickly judge someone she had never met when Athena drew her sword. She raised it over her head. Frantically, I shouted

No, wait

while trying to punch the correct button combination for a blocking spell, but I must have done it wrong, because her sword fell and cleaved Rodric the Retrograde right down the middle, bisecting him neatly and bloodlessly. Just before my headset went dead, I heard Cynthia say

I can kill the Toad by myself.

I yanked off the headset and threw it at Paris, dropped the controller, ignored Paris's indignation as it clattered hard to the ground, and snarled

Thanks a lot, you asshole.

Paris blinked, looking as if he had no idea what I was blabbering about. He said

What did I do? All I did was ask you a question. If Jane of the Jungle is too uptight to take a little joke, you should find another playmate anyway.

Well, it was on from that point. Paris had no idea that his offhand comment would start a war, but that's exactly what happened. From that moment, we shared a common goal—to rob each other of greater and greater *UQ XIX* triumphs. On Paris's next turn, he fought his way into the Golden Drawing Room and was slugging it out with the Minister's Daughter when I accidentally on purpose tripped over his controller wire, yanking it out of his hand at the very moment he was trying to block her spell. His character—Mikey the Milquetoast, a wizard with a decidedly foppish air whose name annoyed me every time I read it—got turned to stone, but Paris had reached a checkpoint only a half hour ago. He didn't have to start over, but I did. Again.

Rather than try to come up with a whole new character—easy for a writer, perhaps, but you can't work all the time—I simply recreated Rodric, using the same characteristics. For two hours I roamed through the tunnels and the swamp; I even managed to find Athena again and tried to apologize, but she nearly decapitated Rodric before I could say anything. I wondered why she was still in the swamp so long after she killed me, but I wasn't about to stick around and ask.

Next I stumbled across a nest of Fire Newts; they all tried to roast me for dinner. They were NPCs, so I had no problem wiping them out. Paris helpfully told me that they could be used for food, which was lucky; Rodric's health meter was running low. But, as soon as Rodric ate, he collapsed, poisoned. I said

I knew it. But I just got past a checkpoint, you big jerk. No more starting over from scratch.

Paris cackled. He yanked the controller out of my hand and started his game again. I went to the kitchen to get some chips and was astonished to see that the clock read 2:13 AM. I glanced uneasily at my cell phone; I had turned it off before we began playing. I turned it back on and checked my messages, hoping for the best. But as I feared, Carol had called four times, leaving as many voicemails. I didn't bother listening to them; I pretty much knew what they'd say. I hesitated, then dialed her number. She picked up on the second ring and said without any preamble

Michael fucking asshole Seymour, where the hell are you? I have been trying to call you for hours

and, raising my voice, I said

I'm at Paris's in Little Rock. Didn't you get my email?

and she said

No, I did not get your email, and why are you shouting?

and I shouted

What? I'm not flouting you, baby. I'm just playing games with Paris. I'll be back sometime tomorrow

and she snarled

No, Michael. You will not stay there overnight playing one of those stupid games

and I shouted

What? Listen, baby, I can barely hear you. We must have a bad connection. I'll be home sometime tomorrow. I love you

and, as she was shouting

Do not hang up this phone

I hung up and turned the phone off again, throwing it on the table as if it were scorching my hands. I returned to the living room with a bag of pretzels and a beer. Paris said

Carol?

and I said

Yeah. I think I got her off my case till at least tomorrow

and began plotting some way to kill Paris's character before he could save again.

But I didn't go home the next day, or the one after that. Paris called in sick and we kept playing *UQ XIX*. I had no one to call in sick to except for my conscience, which was always whispering that I should be writing. I ignored it; since I generally write even on weekends and holidays, I figured that I had earned a break. We ordered more pizza and Chinese takeout and managed to kill each other's characters every couple of hours.

The party lasted until someone knocked on the door four days later. Paris answered, assuming our latest take-out order had arrived. I had finally reached the Emerald Lake and was fighting for my life against an electric eel that was, inexplicably, armed with a mace. It kept swinging the damn thing at me and knocking holes in my boat, which I was having to repair as I fought, a task both difficult and frustrating. I finally managed to disarm it and was about to deliver the killing stroke when I felt a sharp pain in the back of my head. I dropped my controller and fell forward onto my face, my stomach roiling, vision blurred. I felt like I was going to puke all over Paris's floor and shit my pants at the same time, but before I could do either, the world went dark.

I woke up in pain, my head filled with broken glass. Carol was leaning over me, throwing droplets of water in my face. Paris hovered nearby, looking concerned. For the first time in days, the game was silent, the television screen dark. I tried to sit up and the pain exploded in my head, the world turning white. I moaned. Carol snorted. My eyes hurt too much to look at her, but I could almost smell the derision and the satisfaction. I groaned

What happened?

and Carol said

Paris's ceramic vase hit you in the back of the head and you passed out

and I said

Well, who threw the fucking thing at me?

and Carol said

I did.

I managed to open my eyes long enough to look at her. She was glaring at me, obviously pleased with her marksmanship, perhaps still mad enough to hit me again. I decided the best course of action was to grovel at her feet. But, unable to move without great pain, I simply said

Honey, I'm sorry. I've been a jerk

and she stood up, saying

No, you've been an asshole. Jerk is too good for you. I'm going home now. Perhaps you should think about leaving, too, while you still have a life to come back to.

She stood, picked up her purse, and walked out the door without another word. Paris watched her leave, scratching his head. I realized that he really needed a shower. For the first time in days, I wondered how I smelled. He smiled, his teeth a sickly green, and said

She actually tried to throw it at me, but I dodged and it hit you. It's all in the reflexes, I guess.

He sat down beside me, not even bothering to offer me a pillow. His eyes were wild, wide and bloodshot and baggy like a psychotic, ill-kempt raccoon. And as I lay there, moaning and concussed, he turned on the television and picked up the controller again.

A Theatrical Evening

In my defense, I was exhausted. From the book signing in Dallas, I caught a 4:15 flight out of DFW to Little Rock. Then I drove two hours back to my house. I only stopped once, just long enough to grab a Big Mac and a Sprite in Pine Bluff. I was ready to kill Darlene, my agent, for rushing the tour so much; Dallas marked my twelfth city in two weeks. I had done ten radio shows, two local TV interviews, and twelve bookstores, plus one brief appearance on Leno. Darlene told me we were lucky to cram all that publicity into fourteen days; her husband Morrie concurred, the jerk. And he's my editor, so I have to listen to his shit, and he had taken every opportunity to pile it on the whole time. By the time I pulled into my driveway, I just wanted to be alone. I mean, I love my fans. They've stroked my ego, made me rich, built my reputation as a split-the-critics-but-please-the-readers author. But I hate the traveling, putting my life and livelihood in the hands of some probably drunken pilot I've never seen before and will only meet long enough for him to say hello and goodbye, thank you for flying whichever the fuck airline he works for.

And damn, book signing hurts after a while. You've heard of tennis elbow? I get autograph palm. I wish people could be happy with a Hi, how are you or a handshake, but no, everybody wants something permanent. They should study the letters of a famous writer, the kind you find in the dusty archives of a major university library. They'd see that signatures fade. It's all memory, I want to tell them. You have to make it last in yourself. But nobody listens to the truth when it contradicts what they want to hear.

Once I got home, it took me nearly a full minute to fit my key into the front door; the lock kept swimming in front of my eyes, like I was seeing it through a thin scrim of gray ice. My legs felt like someone had fitted them with heavy casts, and my right arm still ached from two weeks of writing my name over and over and over. Once I finally got inside, I threw my bags on the floor, went to my fridge, and took out a beer. I opened it and downed half of it before the cap I tossed aside had stopped rattling on the counter. I carried my bottle into the living room and sat down, not even bothering to turn on a lamp. The light outside had taken on the dusky gray hue of faded sheets, and it bled in through the curtain, providing limited but sufficient visibility. I leaned my head back against the deep cushions of my couch, wishing I had gotten a cold compress for my aching head. But my desire for the cool drip of water on my temples paled against the deep ache in my muscles and bones. Though I had been sitting—in planes, in cabs, in the rack-like hardback chairs the bookstores always seem to provide—I felt as though I had been on my feet for years. Needles of pain arced up from the soles of my feet, settling in the base of my spine like the tiny grass burs that stick in your socks. But I was glad to be home.

I had been home at least an hour before I even noticed the changes. I don't know what that says about me.

I nearly fell asleep sitting up, beer between my legs. I would have regretted it later, when I woke with a super-sized crick in my neck and a pair of frozen balls. For that, at least, I suppose I should be grateful to my girlfriend Carol, who almost made me piss myself by leaping into the room and shouting

Surprise

and I started forward, yelling

Whafukinhell?

and fell off the couch, landing hard on my ass. The shock traveled the length of my spine, notching up the dull ache to a live-wire throb, as the beer bottle flew outward and skittered across my glasstop coffee table, cascading droplets of amber and suds. Carol pranced over and righted the bottle, grabbing some Kleenex from the box on the coffee table and blotting up the beer. Then she stood over me with her arms spread wide, trying not to laugh. I frowned up at her, which only seemed to make her giggle harder, so I upgraded to a scowl. Slowly I stood up, wincing, wishing that I had gotten a Swedish massage at the airport, wondering if DFW even offered that service, intentionally paying as little attention to Carol as possible. I admit that I was a pretty pissed off mass of aches and pains. My early 40s seemed far too early to fall apart physically, but I already felt like an old man. I stretched my back before I sat back down on the couch, my vertebrae popping like bubble wrap under a kid's feet, and said

How about next time you don't scare the shit out of me when I'm almost asleep?

Ignoring both my tone and my pain, she sat down beside me and brushed my hair out of my eyes, rubbed the back of my neck. She said

Sorry. I just wanted to surprise you. It's the first time you've finished a tour on your birthday.

It took a few moments for what she said to sink in. Then I shook her hand away from the nape of my neck and thought hard. Was it my birthday? Had I really forgotten it? Over the last week I had begun telling time in terms of what bookstore and city I was supposed to be in, the cup of tarry coffee I could grab from somebody's ancient percolator, the fancy kimchee-on-lettuce-leaves receptions sometimes provided in lieu of real food. I stood up and slumped over to my calendar, turning it over to the correct month, and counted forward two weeks from the last date I remembered for sure. And there it was, my birthday, marked on the calendar with little red hearts Carol had drawn in with a sharpie. I looked around at her and whistled, low and long. I said

Damn. I completely forgot about it.

She laughed, the polar opposite of the reaction I would have gotten if I had forgotten her birthday instead. I sat back down beside her and sighed heavily. She said

You just need some sleep. Or a really good present.

I grinned and scooted closer to her, taking her hands in mine, leaning in for a kiss, saying

Now you're talking

but she pushed me away, her palms flat against my chest. She said

Not that kind of present, you goofball

and I sat back, feeling annoyed and horny, saying

Well, what is it then?

and she looked hard at me, trying, I think, to see if I were joking. When she had convinced herself that I was serious, she said

You really haven't noticed it yet, have you?

and I said

Noticed what?

She snorted and swept her arm in a semicircle, the gesture taking in the whole of my living room. I looked around. At first the contrast was disconcerting, parts of the room clear, others in shadow, like a scene from a 1940s film noir. But as my eyes adjusted, I saw something new and reached over, turning on the Tiffany lamp on my side table. A new Blu-Ray player sat atop my old DVD machine. Its face was blank, save for a tiny red dot in the upper left corner, probably a power indicator. Excitement fluttered like a moth in my gut. Until now, Carol had steadfastly refused to let me have one, even though I had been hinting for months. I couldn't exactly argue, since she controlled my finances and my technological toys. It was for the best, really. Whereas some people become addicted to drugs or booze or gambling, I'm addicted to technology, even though I find its constant evolution disconcerting and scary. Carol's control made my life less chaotic, and besides, I could blame her for anything bad that happened.

But I wasn't thinking about all that as I crossed the room slowly, never taking my eyes off of the player, as though it might disappear if I looked away. I stood in front of the entertainment center, the HDTV's blank eye staring past me as the light outside faded further toward night. Carol stood beside me, beaming. For the second time, she said

Happy birthday

and I kissed her, hard and long. Images of nights filled with film and featurette and commentary and trailers danced through my head, all of them bursting forth in the colors and vivid lines of high definition. I imagined a huge movie library lining my walls—classics from the Golden Age, the comedies of Woody Allen and Mel Brooks, the entire *oeuvre* of Mel Gibson and Bruce Willis and Arnold Schwarzenegger, whatever had been transferred to Blu-Ray. Even my DVDs would look better. I think I must have been drooling. Then Carol cleared her throat and said

You haven't even noticed the walls, have you?

I followed her gaze, and there, mounted to the wall, hung one of the biggest speakers I had ever seen outside of a rock concert. I said

You mean...?

and Carol said

Yes, you now have surround sound. And look back there.

Two more speakers had been mounted to the wall behind the couch. They were smaller than the others, each about the size of a shoebox. I had been so tired when I came in that I hadn't even noticed them. Still, I felt positively orgasmic, weak in the knees, my lower lip trembling. The possibilities were staggering. I turned to Carol and took her in my arms, planting kisses all over her face and neck, and said

It's the best present I've ever gotten
and she said
I know.

You have to forgive a bit of hubris in a woman who will not only buy but also install a home entertainment system while you're away on business.

She handed me a complicated remote control, one of those with more buttons than an airplane cockpit. I had no idea what to do other than punch the power button, so I did. Nothing happened. I hit it again, still nothing. I shook the remote, hard, and tried again—still nothing. Carol said

You're punching it too fast. It's just like your old DVD remote; you have to point it and hold the button down till it comes on.

She demonstrated, and sure enough it worked. The readout said
No Disc.

Carol took my TV remote and turned the set to its video channel. She mumbled an apology for not getting a universal remote. Now I saw the opening screen, a kind of dark blue haze in the background, the player's logo centered and crisp. I was already making plans for how I might sneak away and buy a bunch of Blu-Ray discs. Then Carol said

I can see that you're planning something. But if it's movies you're worried about, I think I've got that covered.

She walked to the hall and came back pulling a cardboard box damn near big enough to hold a refrigerator. She was using both hands, bending over and wriggling her ass in the air. I offered to help, but she shooed me away. So I watched, curious and amused, as she yanked and rammed the box across the floor. Finally she stopped next to the coffee table. She sat down on the floor, breathing heavily and sweating, and pointed to the box, looking at me with an expression that said
Well?

I shrugged and ripped open the packing tape, expecting to find two Blu-Rays set on top of a load of bricks, one of those cheesy surprise gifts like wrapping a diamond ring in a TV box. But I found that Carol had gone overboard this time. The box was absolutely packed with movies, most still shrink-wrapped with the security strips firmly held in place. I began pulling them out, first one by one and then by twos and threes. She had bought, by my estimate, over two hundred and fifty Blu-Rays. I had every Hitchcock film that had been transferred to the format, including all the biggies like *North by Northwest*, the Stanley Kubrick collection, the Oliver Stones, tons of Woody Allen. I had every Gibson flick I could remember, plus incomplete but impressive runs from Ford, Huston, Capra, Spielberg, and James Cameron. Moreover, she had found not only most of David Fincher's works but also a couple by Ed Wood and Corman, of all people. I had enough films to keep me going for weeks. I know I was drooling then, like a starving man who had stumbled into an all-you-can-eat buffet. Carol told me later that she got up to pee three times while I was looking through the discs. I never noticed.

When I finally came up for air, Carol had ordered take-out from the local steakhouse. The fridge had been stocked with my favorite beer, Shiner Bock. She was thinking of everything. That night I got quietly drunk and way too full while we watched *Annie Hall*, *A Clockwork Orange*, and *Mad Max III: Beyond Thunderdome*. I have no idea why we chose those movies, but they certainly mirrored my decreasing neural activity, from high comedy to biting and bloody satire to a crappy *Road Warrior* suckfest that only appealed to hardcore *Max* fans. Me, I loved every second of it.

When I woke up the next day, mouth desert-dry and head stuffed with wet cotton, I rolled out of bed, groaning. I shaved and brushed my teeth, gargling with enough Listerine to deodorize a bull elephant, trying to disintegrate the dead animal that had somehow crawled into my mouth. I managed to eat a couple of scrambled eggs without barfing. All this exhausted me, so I plopped down on my couch and settled back.

I lay there for a couple of hours, letting the aspirin I had taken work its way through me. I got up twice, once to piss and once to get a bottle of water. Otherwise, I reclined amongst the pillows and the filtered sunlight, enjoying the silence, dozing and shifting the pillows. But soon enough the inside of my head began to feel less like a few dozen professional wrestlers were having a Battle Royal in my brain; my mouth eventually tasted less like fried sheep shit. I sat up, stood, drank another bottle of water. I even felt a bit hungry. I ate some white bread and a few potato chips, savoring the grease and salt.

Wiping crumbs off my shirt, I nestled back down on my couch. My television sat across the room, blank, inert. It was one of my favorite possessions; I could hardly leave it in that condition. I felt bound by honor, by my dedication to the things I loved, to use it as it was made to be used. I had a duty, a sacred trust requiring me to turn it on and watch it. And as long as I was watching it, I might as well take in a movie, or maybe two. Three if I had time.

My problems at this point were twofold. First, I really needed to write. I hadn't gotten any work done in two days, and I had an article for *Slate* on the state of Southern fiction due in a week. I also owed myself twenty pages on the new novel I was writing, since I tried for ten a day. The other part of the problem? Carol. We had a great time watching those movies, even the cheesy ones. It was probably the best birthday I've had since my seventeenth, when Trish Morgenstern blew me in my Mom's station wagon on the way home from a ball game. As it happened, I had promised to wait for Carol so we could do it all again. She had said

After all, if you sit on the couch and watch movies without me all day, you'll get behind on your work and screw up your back even worse.

She was right on both counts. My couch was really comfy, but sitting on it all day, especially in prime movie-watching condition—slumped down against the cushions, neck resting against the edge, knees at right angles, feet spread wide—would be tough on my spine. And dammit, I really needed to get on that article; they were offering to pay me quite well, at least on the freelance writer salary scale. And the novel wouldn't write itself. I sat there for a while, feeling better and better, debating the question. On one side, I could choose hurting my girlfriend's feelings and falling even further behind on the job I loved. On the other, I could pick movies. Lots of movies.

Really, I had no choice, not in the final analysis.

Now, I'm not an asshole. Really. Carol might sometimes argue the point, but I think she'd say that most of my mistakes result from misguidance, not malice. I don't set out to do the wrong thing or hurt people or screw up my life. But it happens anyway. I blame my mother. She always let me have cookies just before supper. That kind of instant gratification couldn't have been good for my personality development, at least that's what my therapist used to say. In any case, I paid my money and I took my choice, as Mom used to say.

I pushed myself off the couch, walked across the room, and turned on the player. I looked at the piles of films surrounding my entertainment center, rising off the floor like geometrical mountains. Perhaps it wasn't too late yet. Perhaps I still had time to fall asleep again, or, better yet, sit down at my computer to write for a few hours. Perhaps I could still save myself a lot of aggravation. I needed a sign, some indication of what I should do. Of course I couldn't trust my own judgment; what had that ever gotten me? I looked around the room, on the walls, out the window where I could see my neighbor mulching her lawn, on the floor—

And I saw it, lying right where I couldn't miss it—my sign. Beautiful in its simplicity, almost frightening in its symbolic weight. It was exactly what I needed—*Evil Dead 2*. On the cover, a grinning skull sported, inexplicably, a pair of staring eyeballs. It is perhaps my favorite movie ever, one of the few films that seems to know how cheesy it really is, that has the guts to make fun of itself and the wit to do it well. From that moment on, I lay in the hands of fate or luck or whatever name you want to give it. And I submitted.

I picked up the case, my knees creaking, head spinning with the remnants of alcohol. The case felt smooth and cool in my hands. When I shifted my grip, I could see my fingerprints on the cover. I had marked it as mine, as it had marked me with its giggling skeletal gaze. I opened the case and took out the disc.

Carol showed up that night around seven, harried and tired. She and her supplier had viciously argued, and though she claimed to have won, we later learned that she was no longer welcome in the city of Dallas. I have no idea how she managed to alienate herself from an entire city after only one telephone conversation, but it was true. We actually tested it not long ago. We flew to DFW and tried to check in at a Marriott using her name and credit card, only to be told that no rooms were available. We hung out for a couple of hours until a new desk clerk arrived, at which time I easily obtained a room, as well as the assurance that they had several vacancies. I guess you just shouldn't piss off some people, especially in the age of email and chat rooms and instant messaging.

On this particular night, with that wound fresh, Carol stomped in my front door as if it had offended her, throwing it open and sending it crashing into the wall, slamming it closed with a bang, the noise so loud that I could scarcely hear Bruce Campbell's commentary track. I was still watching *Evil Dead 2*. I had written not a single word; on the other hand, I had watched only one movie. Three times, true, and I had also taken in most of the special features, but I hadn't indulged any further. Surely, I reasoned, Carol could hardly explode over one little film, especially something loosely connected to the horror genre, which she hated. Surely I was safe, even if my front door and the surrounding walls were not.

As usual, though, I had reckoned without Carol's particular brand of righteous indignation, which, in anyone else, I might be tempted to term bitchiness. I just don't get her sometimes. I mean, here I am, a relatively famous and somewhat critically lauded author, a guy who makes enough money to take care of us both for the rest of our lives. I don't ask much of her, and I allow her ridiculous levels of control. I can't get on my own goddam computer and log onto the Internet without her permission. She buys everything for me. My books have financed her entire decorating scheme and the landscaping of her yard. Hell, she rents her mother an apartment in Pine Bluff and pays for it out of my accounts, and do I say anything? No, I don't. I keep quiet like a five-year-old who's been bad and knows he shouldn't piss Mommy off any worse. So silly me, I didn't think that it was asking too much on the rare occasion when I took a full day off from writing and watched one of my own movies.

Naturally, I was wrong, as I am about so many things. I often wonder what my readers would say if they knew just how bad I am with simple, everyday things. Perhaps I wouldn't have been a finalist for the National Book Award. Perhaps no one would come to my readings. Perhaps no one would buy my books. Or perhaps they'd simply agree that Carol can be a bitch, that she overreacts, that she sometimes seems to wait for me to make a tiny mistake so she can take out all her frustrations on me, and that my saying all this out loud doesn't make me a misogynist. I'd hope so, anyway.

She stomped into the living room and saw what was on the television, Bruce Campbell frozen in an expression of mock rage as I paused the film. I dropped the remote on the couch; it immediately fell between the cushions, as remotes are wont to do, and I jumped up like I had been jabbed with a needle, running to her, kissing her on the cheek, asking

What's wrong, baby? Bad day at work?

She glared at me, cold, furious. I knew I was in trouble. She said

Michael. What are you doing? You promised that you would wait for me. You are watching a movie. You broke your promise and you've ruined the evening I've planned

and I said

Ruin how? I can turn this off anytime. I just didn't feel like writing today, baby, and you know how it is. If you aren't feeling it, you're just beating your head against a wall. You can't force creativity

and she said

Michael, you can't possibly know whether you can write or not until you actually, you know, try to write. You are watching this film because you have no respect for me or what I want.

Now, I confess that I don't always handle things in the most productive way. Everybody knows that about me. So I suppose no one would be surprised to learn that, instead of figuring out the best way to calm her down and thus defuse the situation, I simply got mad. I mean, I love Carol and all, but I was thinking to myself, who the hell does she think she is, telling me now that I can't even watch a fucking movie in my own house? So I said

How the bloody hell can you say that when you control my every move and I don't say a damn thing nine times out of ten? I'm not rebelling against your precious authority or trying to hurt your feelings. I'm just watching a movie, Carol

and she said

It's not just a movie. It's a symbol. It shows how you don't respect me or anything else except what you want. You're like a baby

and I said

Well, I guess it's a good thing for me that you apparently think you're my goddam mother.

I don't really remember much after that.

I woke up five minutes later, my head feeling like a broken pumpkin, a sharp pain in my hand. I looked to my right and saw that I had cut myself rather badly on a patch of jagged glass. I sat up and began picking shards out of my fingers, trying to understand what had happened to me. Little by little I was able to think again, and I realized that the glass embedded in my hand had once comprised my favorite lamp, one that Carol herself had given me, heavy glass base and tan, bead-fringed shade. Its remains lay on the carpet beside me like a half-buried fossil. Even the bulb had broken. Carol was gone.

She must have brained me with the damn thing sometime after I compared her to my mother. What was worse, I might have said other, even stupider things that I now cannot remember. I felt horrible, and not just because I was suffering from a filleted hand and a possible concussion. Sure, Carol had come on too strong, had blown a moment of selfishness out of proportion. But as usual, I shot off my fool mouth, opening it as widely as possible and sticking not just my foot but my entire leg in it, all the way up to the hip, as apt a mixed metaphor as I have ever written.

I got a bath towel out of the hall closet and staggered to my master bathroom. I opened the medicine cabinet and took out a bottle of alcohol, opening it with my left hand while holding it in the crook of my right arm. My right hand was bleeding all over my clothes, the floor, the counter. I was turning the whole place into a Jackson Pollock painting. Steeling myself, I poured the alcohol over my hand. The pain was immediate and intense, fire in my arm, my nerve endings cursing me as thoroughly and as loudly as Carol undoubtedly had. I wrapped the towel around my hand, watching as the blood blossomed forth in eerie, artistic patterns.

I weaved drunkenly back to the living room and sat on the couch, noticing for the first time that the lamp represented only a small part of the destruction. Carol had thrown something through the television; the gaping hole glared at me like the shark's eyes in *Jaws*, one of my favorite films, the same one that was now broken in half and resting on the coffee table like a ruined saucer still waiting for a cup. One of the new speakers hung askew on the wall, as if Carol had kicked it really hard without managing to dislodge it; the other was lying on its face on the floor, like the body in *The Trouble with Harry*, another disc lying broken, this one under the table.

Not all the discs were ruined, of course. She hadn't had time. But she had trashed quite a few and had thrown the rest around the room helter skelter. Now it wasn't just the light that made my living room look like a detective's office in a noir picture, the kind where the villains break in and toss the place, looking for the photos or the documents or the whatever-the-hell. My hand ached; my head pounded. And I couldn't even watch a movie to forget about it.

The Handy Helper

I remember the falling tree branch, like a movie point-of-view shot where something hurtles toward the camera and you wonder how they ever got the take. I heard creaking from somewhere above me, like a rusty door being opened slowly and deliberately. Then the branch snapped off and fell, smashing me to the ground. I remember a brief moment of pain and bright shapes flashing across my mind—not stars, but I could see why people use that cliché when they've been hit on the head, explosions of geometry and then darkness deeper than sleep. I'd say that I have no idea how long I lay there beside Parrott Pond, but I can tell you exactly because of the Handy Helper. That was the only use I could find for the goddam thing on that long, long weekend.

This whole sad chapter in my life began with a phone call from my girlfriend Carol, as so many of them seem to do. I was eating a late lunch with my best friend Dray, around 2:30 I'd guess; his favorite soap opera, *Rocky Hills,* had just ended, but I was still making fun of him for watching, so it couldn't have been much later. We were sitting in Frederica's, a mom and pop diner on Main Street, within walking distance from the Parkview Post Office and the city jail. We had been arguing over the relative merits of curling, that stupid Canadian sport in which a broom represents the equipment of choice. Occasionally we'd see a mail truck or police car go by and we'd stop arguing long enough to watch, wondering who or what was being delivered to where. And just as I was preparing to nail Dray with my best and most thoughtful argument for why curling was the most useless sport this side of spitting contests, my cell phone rang. I jumped, knocking over my half-empty glass of iced tea, the remainder darting as if sentient toward Dray's side of the table and spilling over the edge, soaking him, the dark stain on his pants the approximate shape of Ontario. He cursed throughout my whole conversation, which would have been funny had we not been sitting next to a Baptist minister and a Catholic priest, who had for the last fifteen minutes been giggling at each other's dirty jokes.

It was Carol, of course. Who else would it be? She always managed to call my cell at the most inopportune times—when I was driving in heavy traffic or taking a shit or flirting with some other woman. She never would have called had she known I'd spill tea all over Dray; those two have always been close and have spent the last few years allied against me. Not long ago I realized that the town had installed a traffic camera in the red light on north Main Street—nobody else believes this, but I know it's true—and Carol feared I was having another paranoid episode, so she and Dray browbeat me into taking Elm for a month. You'd think a grown man could pick his own routes, but I can't. I have to consult my Life Committee first.

Anyway, I answered the phone, though I was almost laughing too hard to speak. I said something like

He-heh-heh-heh-ell-oooo

and Carol said

Mike? What the hell?

and, trying to calm down, I said

Sorry, I just soaked Dray's crotch, and he's dancing around Frederica's like his feet are on fire

and she said

I don't even want to know. Listen, I bought a new PDA, so if you want my old Handy Helper, I'll bring it over

and I said

Carol, we've talked about this. I don't want your old Handy Helper. I have no use for a PDA. I make do just fine with pens and Post-Its

and she said

And how many of those notes have floated off your fridge? You've missed I don't know how many of our lunches because you forgot about them. What else have you missed?

Well, a lot, actually, but I wasn't about to tell her that. I once missed my mother's birthday party because I went out drinking with my editor, and one day I was supposed to be in Dallas for a book signing and ended up in Tijuana with four hookers and a dentist. But what I said was

Look, I gotta go; Dray just ran out of the building and I think

Frederica's going to call the cops if I don't pay the check.

I hung up and paid, telling Frederica that Dray suffered from a bladder control problem and acute schizophrenia. Not very interested, she nodded and took my twenty bucks. I left and got in my car, chasing Dray down the street and calling

You dumbass, if you'll just get in, I'll drive you home.

He finally stopped running and climbed in, glaring at me. We drove to his house in relative silence, the only sounds being James Taylor's Sweet Baby James on the radio and my incessant giggling. Dray scowled the whole way, and his discomfort amused me so much that I didn't think about Carol and her Handy Helper at all.

But Carol didn't forget; she never forgets anything. She still remembers the birthdays of friends she made in first grade, while I barely remember the name of my school. I got home that night and there she stood, making red beans and rice in my kitchen, the air heavy with the curry powder she insists on putting in everything but breakfast cereals, and on my kitchen table sat the Handy Helper, its screen glowing a sickly green, as if someone had blown radioactive snot all over it. Carol stopped stirring the pot and ran up to me, grasping me around the waist and squeezing as if she hadn't seen me in days. I gasped for breath, my eyes watering from the pressure and spices, but I let her squeeze, her breasts mashing pleasantly against my chest. I kissed her on the forehead and said

How was your day?

and she said

Let's eat. I'm starving.

So, after a hearty dinner in which I ate far too much and contracted a terrible, chest-bursting case of heartburn, Carol sat down beside me on my couch, Handy Helper in hand. She said

Now, honey, let me show you how this little baby is going to simplify your life.

In my experience, those words never lead to anything good.

I'm addicted to technology, but I also fear it; there's something ominous about how machines are taking over our lives, one credit card scanner or digital camera at a time. I love devices that I can use without changing the way I live my life at its most basic, intimate level. So anytime Carol tells me that some gadget can affect everything I know, I run like a hooker at a Baptist convention. The problem is that she can outwait me. She knows how long it will take me to cave in. She also finds ways to chisel away at my resolve, like saying

Hey, did you know you can use this thing to write notes? If you have an idea for a story while you're driving down the road, just pull over and put it in

ignoring me completely when I come back with

Okay, but what do I do with that microcassette recorder I bought for the exact same reason?

I eventually figured out the easiest thing to do: take the stupid Handy Helper and pretend to use it. So after two hours, in which time I did not get to watch three TV shows that I had looked forward to all week, I finally said

You know, babe, you may have something there. Why don't you just show me how to turn it on and I'll figure it out from there?

It worked like a charm. I ended the conversation, made her happy, and got laid later that night. And though the Handy Helper lay on my kitchen table, sleek and portentous and annoying, I was happy, for a while.

Of course, Carol had to ruin it two days later by asking me how I liked the goddam thing. I had barely thought about it. For the most part, the Handy Helper did seem pretty cool; its features were staggering, considering the size. I could imagine uses for its calendar, its address book, its Internet capabilities. But then my technophobia kicked in and I remembered how I had been forced to buy every kind of software I could find to protect my computer privacy—virus scanners and cookie removers and spam filters. I didn't think they made similar programs for Handy Helper email and was afraid to ask, knowing that Carol would use the occasion to rant and rave about my alleged paranoia. She was always saying things like that, sometimes even behind my back.

The upshot is that I had dropped the Handy Helper on my bedside nightstand, turned off, hidden underneath the dust jacket of the latest Digby Darrymore borefest and a wad of used Kleenex. So when Carol asked about it, I said

Oh, it's okay. I haven't really had much time to play around with it

and, raising her eyebrows, Carol said

Oh really. Well I happen to know that you've been playing video games with Dray and watching Dr. Phil every afternoon, so how busy could you possibly be?

Now here's what you have to understand. Carol and I have these conversations all the time. She wants me to do something I don't want to do; I lie about having done it; she gets pissy and calls me on it; I lie some more; and the cycle continues until either she gets mad and leaves or I say something really dumb that starts an even worse fight. Our cycle usually lasts about three days. We fight; we don't speak, choosing instead to send cryptic and vaguely threatening messages through third parties like Dray; we make up. We enjoy approximately three days of peace. Then we fight for three more. We therefore argue one-hundred-eighty-two-and-one-half days a year, one-hundred-eighty-three on leap years. Some people have asked us why we don't just break up. I don't know if it's because we're so in love or because we're both too stubborn to admit we've wasted all this time. Having never reached an armistice, we've always been one careless word away from a new explosion. So when she took her sarcastic, I'm-ready-for-my-fight-now-please-sir tone, I responded with

Gosh, I'm really sorry, baby. I guess I didn't realize that accepting ownership of a device I didn't want in the first place would require me to give up all the things I enjoy until such time as I master it to your satisfaction.

One of my neighbors later told me that you could hear our voices two blocks away. Somebody probably would have called the police if we weren't so entertaining.

So the Handy Helper had already aggravated the crap out of me. Carol and I didn't speak for two days, and when she finally called me, it was only to ask if I were still planning my trip to Parrott Pond, the fishing hole five miles or so due west of Parkview. Dray and I had decided to camp out there for a weekend, do some fishing, refuse to bathe, get away from writing and accounting long enough to make it all bearable again. Don't get me wrong; I love writing. But I had been having trouble with my new novel, about a priest who discovers that one of his parishioners is selling dispensations out of an old wood-paneled station wagon. I couldn't decide whether the priest should demonstrate a distaste for the car itself or only for the sinful act; personality quirks like that often haunt me as I write, and I've never been able to get over it and just tell the story. For his part, Dray had just survived another exhausting tax season. We wanted to get away from work and Carol and Dray's nagging aunt who lived next to him with ten cats and a pair of rumble fish, to go someplace that had nothing to do with words or calculating long columns of numbers. But we didn't want to drive very far, and we couldn't just stay home, where people could find us and ask us to run errands or fix stuff. So we had decided that three days and two nights at Parrott Pond were just what we needed.

When Carol called, suspicion ached like a spider bite at the base of my skull. Less than three days had passed since the fight, which meant she was still mad at me, which meant she might be trying to ruin the trip. So I said

We haven't really talked about it, but as far as I know it's still on. Why?

and she said

Because I want you to take the Handy Helper

and I said

Oh, for God's sake, Carol

and she said

Look, I don't want to argue with you. But you're going out in the middle of nowhere. You might get lost or hurt yourselves. Take it, even if you don't use it.

This new tactic puzzled me. She never gave up that easily. Hell, she hadn't even nagged; she had almost phrased it as a request. Naturally I couldn't imagine any situation at Parrott Pond in which a Handy Helper would come in, well, handy. You'd think that I would have learned by now: Carol and Dray are always right. I'm always wrong. I disobey them at my own peril. So what did I do?

If you're thinking that I left the Helper on my nightstand, you're wrong. I did take it with me to Parrott Pond. I carried it in my knapsack, unloaded it in the tent, kept it on the floor beside my cot. It was fully charged.

Yet ultimately, I lay on the banks of Parrott Pond, head split open, blood drying on my face, a broken tree branch lying across my chest, the Handy Helper on the ground beside me, winking in the sun like a mischievous lover.

Dray and I parked on the shores of Parrott Pond at 5:23 PM that Friday. I knew the exact time not only because of my overspecialized, thirty-seven-feature atomic watch and not only because of the dashboard clock—which didn't work anyway, due to a little accident in a hayfield late one night—but because the Handy Helper told time as well. I did not consult my cell phone, having left it at home. We were trying to avoid calls from Darlene the Agent and Morrie the Editor and Dray's mother and any clients who might have gotten an audit notice. I didn't take my portable DVD player or any handheld video games. But I took the Handy Helper because Carol asked me to. If that doesn't prove to everybody that I love her, I don't know what will.

Unfortunately, we left too much at home. Around dusk that first day, we realized that we had no can opener, which was going to make eating our beans and franks rather difficult. So Dray volunteered to drive back to town and get one. I was perfectly okay with that, having settled down on my cot for a nap, mosquito net drawn, nobody around for miles, only the crickets and frogs and birds yammering outside the tent to keep me company. Dray drove away in my SUV, hollering

I'll be back in an hour, two at the most

while I ignored him. As far as I was concerned, he could take his time.

Now comes the part of the story where I have to inject a little of what we in the writing profession call dramatic irony. This particular case seems even more ironic than usual because I'm both the narrator and the character who was unaware of the events occurring across town. Writing about your own past creates these little pockets of postmodern meta-experience.

While I was napping, blissfully dreaming of, if I remember correctly, Carol and Meg Ryan and a vat of chocolate fudge, Dray was leaving Wal-Mart over in Pinedale, having elected to go buy a new can opener instead of just getting one from his house. Dray's weird that way; he doesn't like to chance losing his stuff, even the easily replaceable crap like manual can openers. He pulled out of the parking lot and turned left onto Main Street, stopping at the red light on Main and Fourth. He waited patiently at the light, killing time by changing all my radio settings to country stations. He thought it would be funny, considering that I hate country music.

But Dray gets a taste of dramatic irony in this story, too. Neither he nor I knew that a nasty fate was barreling toward him at that very moment. One Mr. John R. Cowell, an out-of-work bicycle repairman and security guard, was charging down Fourth at approximately fifty miles per hour, and as usual, he was stoned. To tell you the truth, I'm not sure that the brain of John R. Cowell, ex-security guard, fired enough synapses to light a forty-watt bulb, much less help him drive a car. As he careened along Fourth, a residential street, he seemed completely oblivious to the shouts of

Slow down, you asshole

and the wails of the children whose dog he obliterated, its intestines dragging behind his car like blasphemous tassel. John R. Cowell was not a bad man by nature; his life's experiences had simply led him to this point, wherein his only concern was getting to McDonald's for a sixteen-piece McNugget meal with barbecue sauce. He was still accelerating when he passed the intersection of Fourth and Watercress, massacring a squirrel that had been eating a hickory nut in the middle of the road. If he noticed the red light, he paid it no mind. Perhaps he thought it was an acid flashback.

As for Dray, he had turned up my radio, the better to hear Garth Brooks or Toby Keith. He never heard the squealing tires of John R. Cowell's beaten-up piece of shit, never thought to look toward Fourth and make sure that a stoned ex-bicycle repairman wasn't flying toward him like a heat-seeking missile. Dray simply hit the gas when the light turned green and eased across Fourth, heading for the highway that would take him out of Pinedale and toward Parrott Pond, where his cot sat just across from me. For my part, I slept like a dead man.

John R. Cowell turned hard to the right as he hit Main Street, the rear end of his car fishtailing toward Dray. I don't know what happened at that point and Dray doesn't remember, but I can imagine it.

Dray glances to his left and sees an ex-security guard's car sliding toward him at full speed, black smoke rolling off the balding tires and sputtering out of the tailpipe, the rear windshield panning closer, revealing more and more of itself until it looms as large as a movie screen, John R. Cowell still oblivious to Dray's presence. Dray shouts

Oh, fuck

and slams on the gas, my engine roaring to life, my tires shrieking in harmony with John R. Cowell's, but too late, the rear bumper of Cowell's rattletrap smashing into my driver's side door, crushing it inward, metal jutting violently through the padding. The shattered door rams into Dray's left arm, slicing it open with surgical precision, the impact throwing Dray to his right, the seatbelt catching hard and breaking two of his ribs, the air bag deploying, its cover exploding and breaking Dray's nose and left orbital bone, his right leg crashing against the bottom of the dash, breaking his femur just above the knee. Both vehicles spin and careen off of each other again, my SUV tipping over and skidding across Main Street, sparks showering the road, rooster-tailing like fireworks. Some of these flying sparks travel as far as the initial point of impact, where a puddle of gasoline sends rivulets in all directions, though mainly trailing after its source, the car of John R. Cowell, ex-bicycle repairman and security guard. The gasoline ignites and the flames race toward the car, as witnesses on Main Street dive for cover. John R. Cowell's car bursts into flame and, seconds later, explodes, raining debris and pieces of John R. Cowell on the roofs of nearby businesses. Meanwhile, my SUV—wrapped like a cocoon around Dray's unconscious body—skids toward the sidewalk, hits the curb, and jolts to a stop, the hood smashing into a fire hydrant and breaking it open, water erupting, soaking everyone. Before the accident is more than two minutes old, the ambulances are en route. And I am still asleep, dreaming of bringing Meg Ryan to orgasm in a deli while Carol and Billy Crystal watch, awestruck and jealous.

Obviously, Dray didn't return that night. But I didn't notice until almost ten the next morning. I had sprawled on my cot intending to take nothing more than an hour's nap. Instead, I slept straight through the night, around fifteen hours. A lot of people don't realize how hard my job is; they figure that since I'm not digging a ditch in the summer sun or drilling for oil somewhere offshore, I must have it easy. And as far as physical labor goes, I probably do. But most white-collar workers will tell you that there's more than one kind of labor and more than one kind of stress. Creativity is rewarding, but draining; the drafting and revision process can be exciting, but it's also often frustrating and monotonous. Then there's the travel, the arguments with your editors and agents, the interviews with people who want to know where your ideas come from. I hadn't taken a full day off since the last time I went to Little Rock to play video games with my friend Paris. So when I lay down for my short nap, I didn't even consider that I was giving my exhausted mind its first break in the months since I had begun writing the new book.

I remember waking up at one point and hearing something moving out in the woods, but I wasn't worried. Southeast Arkansas isn't known for its large predators, unless you count rednecks. So I fell back asleep. When

I stepped out of the tent that morning, the sunlight slatting through the trees in brilliant bars, I felt refreshed, shocked at how much time had passed and badly needing to take a piss, but feeling better than I had in months.

My SUV was still gone. I thought at first that Dray had simply left again, perhaps for some more beer or ice or a book of matches. We were always forgetting something, needing more of something else. But as the dullness of sleep gradually faded and I started to see with my mind as well as my eyes, I could tell that he had never come back at all. The fire hadn't been tended. I poked my head back into the tent; his bedding had not been disturbed. Our cooking equipment was still packed away. Nothing looked different. If his cot hadn't been stowed in the tent, no one could have seen that he had ever been in camp at all.

I didn't know what had happened or what I should do about it. I was stuck several miles outside of town and wasn't looking forward to walking back; neither was I particularly inclined to stay. I had gone fifteen hours without food, and my stomach was grumbling, roiling, trying to eat itself. I rummaged in our supplies and found some crackers. I began stuffing them into my mouth three at a time, crumbs raining down on my chest like snowflakes. Those saltines were among the most delicious things I've ever eaten, though I almost choked once and had to stop long enough to find a bottle of water.

After I had eaten half the box, I put the rest of the crackers away and sat down outside the tent. The ground and the air both felt like wet skin in a cool breeze, though that would soon change; the sun was climbing high into the sky, the glare bouncing off the pond and directly into my eyes. I still felt pretty good, but now worry trickled through me, puddling up in the back of my mind. For all I knew, Dray was sitting in a Jacuzzi with four busty blondes and a bottle of fine wine. I, however, was all alone, with very little food and a fire that was mostly a memory. I felt safe enough, but man, I hate long walks.

The coals were still glowing underneath a thick layer of ash, so I decided to rebuild the fire and see if I could find something besides snacks. If Dray weren't back by nighttime, I'd put out the fire and start humping back to town, at which point I'd track him down and slap him upside his head.

As this plan was forming, Dray was being wheeled out of surgery. The doctors had managed to repair the shorn tendons in his arm. Dray would lie in a hospital bed for eight days before his grousing forced the doctors to release him, after which he would occupy my guest room for three months, pissing and moaning the whole time.

Back at Parrott Pond, I opened a can of Spam—thank God for pull tabs—and fried it in a skillet. Then I got the bread and made five sandwiches, spreading mayo on them and trying to pretend I was eating a steak and cheese from south Philly. The sandwiches still tasted like the bottom of an old basketball shoe. I don't know how people eat that shit by choice, nor do I have any idea why Dray would have packed it—probably just to annoy me. It worked, too. But I had nothing else besides some sliced lunchmeat, and I wanted to save that in case I had to eat a whole meal by myself again.

At least I got full, even if the food sucked. I opened a bottle of beer and drank it down by the pond, my toes in the water. Mud squelched up between them, which I believe to be one of life's most pleasant sensations. The sun felt warm on my face; the air smelled as if it had been freshly-laundered. Now I actually hoped that Dray wouldn't hurry back, since he would undoubtedly list all the specials he had found at Wal-Mart, the cheap bastard. Somewhere in the woods, a couple of squirrels chattered away at each other. A blackbird landed on the ground not ten feet from me. We stared at each other for a while before he flew off again, leaving me and the pond to ourselves.

But three hours later, I got worried. Dray had never stayed gone that long, no matter what. If nothing else, he would have been itching to show off his woodsmanship, all the little skills he learned in the Boy Scouts while I was writing stories and sneaking my Dad's beer out of the fridge. Yet there was still no sign of him. I couldn't even remember hearing any vehicles pass by, no heavy trucks whose engine noises carried this far away from the main road. That couldn't have been right, of course; most likely my growing sense of alarm had crept up my spine like a hairy and poisonous bug, chewing up my perceptions and leaving only the certainty that I had been forgotten, that something had happened to Dray. I cursed our stupid cell phone rule, Dray's theoretical carelessness, the pond, the blackbird that had flown off and left me.

Then I remembered the Handy Helper. And its email function.

I shouted

Yes

and ran into the tent. I dove onto the floor and began tossing the bedding over my head, throwing my clothes under the cots, ruffling through my sleeping bag. It had to be there somewhere. I finally located it underneath my duffle bag, and how it got there, I'll never know. I'd swear that Dray snuck back into camp and hid it there, but since he lay in a hospital bed, heavily medicated and half-dead at the time, it couldn't have been him. The bastard. He won't even give me the satisfaction of easy explanations.

I yanked the Helper out from under the bag and started tapping the screen, scrolling through menus. I wanted to send a message to Carol and another to Dray, telling her to come get me, telling him that he should have a great time with my car, at least until I could report it stolen. But as I tapped that screen and scrolled through those options, I could not find anything that said email or Internet. Nothing at all.

Frantically, I rifled through my bags again, chunking my underwear and t-shirts and spare socks all over the tent. I dug through Dray's junk—his duffle, his briefcase, his sleeping bag, even the mattress on his cot. If he had been lying there, I'd have reached into his pockets and down his pants.

But I found nothing. No matter how many times I went through everything, I came up empty. I had to face facts: not only was I stuck at the pond with very little food I could actually open, not only was I incommunicado save for the possibilities of the Handy Helper I didn't know how to use, but I had also neglected to pack the instruction booklet. I could see it sitting right where I had left it—in my master bathroom, wedged between an old copy of *Hustler* and a *People* magazine with Bruce Campbell on the cover. I hadn't even bothered to read the damn booklet on the shitter.

I shouted

Mother fucker

and kicked Dray's cot. It clattered for half a second and then came to rest, making more noise than I had heard since Dray left. The silence that rushed back in the wake of my tantrum frightened me more than the possibility that something might have happened to my best friend; it reminded me that I was completely, totally alone. I could walk to town without much trouble, but if you were a writer, would you want to walk five miles down a highway after what happened to Stephen King?

So I could wait and see if someone showed up or try to hitch a ride. I wasn't crazy about those choices. Parrott Pond's usual clientele consisted of drunk campers, stoners, and teenagers looking to get laid. And hitching just isn't safe anymore. If the hitcher isn't a psycho with a machete, the driver just might be.

While I was figuring things out, I decided to make myself useful and gather some firewood. I figured that if Dray did come back, we could salvage the rest of the weekend, and if he didn't, well, it wouldn't hurt to help out the next guy. If nothing else, it would pass the time, so I started puttering around the pond, gathering twigs and a few small branches. I had slipped the Handy Helper into my back pocket, thinking I might try to dope it out later.

And that was when the branch dropped on my head. I was standing under a tree, examining some sticks to see if they were dry enough to burn, when I heard the creaking above me. I looked up just as the creak metamorphosed into a loud snap, like someone had fired a .22 pistol. And I should have run, should have jumped out of the way, should have done anything but what I actually did—I looked up. I can imagine how the scene must have looked, had anyone been around to see. I probably resembled Wile E. Coyote. You know what happens to him. He's in the middle of some convoluted scheme when a shadow encircles him, and it gets bigger and bigger, and you hear this faint whistling noise that rises until it rips right into your head and the shadow takes up the whole screen. Wile E. turns to the camera and holds up a sign that says

mother

and then he's squished flat as a manhole cover, the piano or anvil or rock heavier than fate.

The branch struck me directly in the face, smashing into the bridge of my nose, crushing it. I wouldn't be able to breathe well for months, and not without a septoplasty. A jagged stick ripped through my cheek and damn near broke my teeth. The biggest, meatiest section smashed into my forehead and knocked me out cold. I remember watching the branch hurtle toward me, the limbs twisted like the terrible claws of some creature ripped out of my nightmares. Sharp red pain tore through my head, and then I was dreaming of a feather bed I once slept in as a child. It was soft and warm, like I had been swallowed by a bird and was curled up waiting to be digested.

When I awoke, the branch was still lying on top of me. My mouth and face felt like they had been sliced up with a razor and doused with rubbing alcohol; my head was a barrel stuffed with cotton. Something was crawling on me, tiny legs tickling me like the tips of a thousand feathers, and as I became more alert, I felt pinpricks up and down my body, even the undersides of my feet. I raised my head; somebody shoved a spike through the top of it and I moaned, knowing that I couldn't move and I couldn't stay where I was. It felt like I was being eaten alive. I sat up again, shoving the branch away and trying to ignore the lightning in my head, slapping at my limbs and torso.

Nearby, the Handy Helper lay on the ground, an off-white blur in the corner of my eye. I can't speculate on how it landed seven or eight feet from me, unscathed, while I got creamed by the branch from hell. But there it was, taunting me with its manufactured perfection, as I lay broken and bleeding under a piece of firewood.

The world spun, crazy and out of control; I had to sit still for three or four minutes before everything calmed down and I was reasonably sure I wasn't going to puke. That's when I realized that the back of my head hurt far worse than my face, like someone had punched the top of my spine over and over. I touched the tender, pulsing spot; fresh pain shot through my skull. My hair felt matted and wet. I stood up, my legs wobbly; it was like trying to walk on stilts made of yarn. Once I had more or less steadied myself, I looked down and saw the exposed root that had nearly punched through the back of my skull. I was lucky to be alive.

The Handy Helper still lay in the grass, winking at me in the bright sunlight.

I walked over to it and carefully bent to pick it up. I thought for a minute that I would topple right onto my head, after which my unconscious body would have probably slid right into Parrott Pond. But I managed to grasp the Helper and stand back up without passing out.

The Helper's clock told me that I had been unconscious for two hours, give or take.

An ant crawled across my hand, and I knew what was pricking my legs and torso. Parrott Pond was still, like a puddle in somebody's driveway. Somewhere nearby a bird sang, its voice high-pitched and reedy like a drunk's. I walked slowly, one halting step at a time, into the pond, still holding the Handy Helper. The brackish water covered my feet, my shins; when it reached my chin, I stopped. The pond was cold; soon my teeth chattered with a sound in my head like firecrackers. Ants floated around me, kicking and struggling. Some crawled into my hair, but I was afraid to duck my wounded head underwater, so they were safe. I stood there for a while, letting the ants wash away, the water prickling the stings.

After a while, I let the Handy Helper go, feeling it brushing my thigh and foot as it floated to the bottom and settled somewhere in the muck. I couldn't see the little cloud of mud that puffed around it as it landed, but I could feel it, knew that tiny particles of sediment were even now peppering the Handy Helper's surface, some immediately brushed away in the current, some remaining, steadfast, like shells on the beach. As far as I know, the Helper's still down there, buried in the sediment like treasure. I've often wondered what a future archaeologist will make of it when she finds it near the bones of southeast Arkansas bream and fossilized birch leaves.

The Classroom

Ever since I published my first book, I've met fans who can quote me verbatim, who memorize release dates, who remember characters' birthdays. But some things are still secret. Some things, nobody knows. For instance, almost nobody knows that I once taught a class at the University of Southeast Arkansas. I lasted one semester. I'm not proud of what happened; I hate to admit it, but my work there is considered something of a disgrace. The whole thing might be funny if it weren't so damn disturbing.

It all started one day at lunch. I was eating a ham sandwich on rye with too much mustard. It had oozed out of the bread and down my fingers, puddling on my Dockers. I shouted

Goddammit

and threw the sandwich down, mustard coating my hand, the wet spots on my pants cold against my skin. I leapt up, hands held out to my sides like a gunfighter, looking for a napkin or paper towel, and of course I saw nothing but the tablecloth. I cried

Carol

hoping she could hear me over the television. She was lying on the couch and watching her soap opera, a piece of badly written shit called *Rocky Hills*. I hated that show. The characters always had the same conversations over and over again, never moving on with their lives, never solving their problems. You'd think that any moron could learn how to deal with their friends and lovers after so much trial and error, but no; they just moved from story to story, spinning their wheels, never learning a goddam thing. Still, unless she had a lunch meeting somewhere, Carol never missed it, and she usually watched it at my house. I think she just liked to see the look on my face whenever I'd catch a snippet of the contrived dialogue or the scenery-chewing reaction shots.

She didn't hear me shouting at her because Shelbi, the pregnant twentysomething heiress with two different lovers and an evil stepfather who was plotting to blow up the town hall, was shouting at her younger sister, who had just recently emerged from a coma. You can tell how that would seem more important than real-life crises like mine, right? So I staggered toward the bathroom, mustard sliding down my pants in thin rivulets. I cursed my sandwich and Carol and myself and the mustard manufacturers and the writers of *Rocky Hills*. Soon I was elbow deep in soap and water, my pants puddled on the floor beside me, and at that very moment the phone rang, not my cell but the house line, one phone in the kitchen and one in my bedroom. The bathroom was equidistant from both, and so, wet and half naked, I prayed that Carol would hear the phone and pick it up. And naturally she shouted

Michael, will you please get that? I'm watching my show.

It happens that way every time.

I grabbed the phone on its ninth ring, out of breath and still wet to the elbows, panting

Hello

but I heard only the low insectile buzz of the dial tone.

Ten minutes later, the phone rang again. I was ready this time. In fact, I had been standing beside it, staring at it, willing it to ring. I yanked it off the charger and barked

Hello

before I even got the receiver to my ear, giving whoever was on the other end no time to back out again. I needn't have worried, though. I heard a voice burst into laughter and then say

Geez, Mike, it's called decaf. Check it out sometime.

The voice belonged to Darlene, the ballsy redheaded agent who had helped make me a rich man. She always got top dollar for my work, whether she was dealing with my editor Morrie, who happened to be her husband, or with miserly film producers. I liked her a lot and owed her even more, but when my dander is up, it stays that way for everybody. So I said

Was that you who called me and hung up ten minutes ago? If so, you dragged me out of the bathroom, where I was taking a particularly good dump.

This was a lie, of course, but I couldn't let her feel too comfortable.

I hoped for a disgusted intake of breath or a derisive snort, but she ignored me. She said

The reason I called. You've just been offered a rather unusual gig that I think you should take. How'd you like to teach college?

I thought Darlene had lost her mind. Asking me to teach college is like asking your four-year-old to organize receipts for that upcoming tax audit. Not that I'm slow or immature—you wouldn't apply such descriptions to a National Book Award finalist, at least not very often. No, I'm pretty intelligent and grown-up, for the most part. But I always hated school and could never really accomplish much while I was there. If the teacher told me to work a math problem, I'd get halfway through it and then start drawing little boats in the margins of my notebook. If I were supposed to be reading one of Shakespeare's plays, I'd go over to somebody's house and act out all the swordfights, skipping over the speeches entirely. And I liked Shakespeare. School always bored me to death. I thought about issues that none of my classmates—or my teachers—cared about, like whether the astronauts who landed on the moon could see the Rocky Mountains. I'd think of what it must have been like, floating around on the chalky surface, exploring craters, while school kids recited their perfect tenses over and over and over and over. I always thought I was made for better, greater things. So asking me to go back in a classroom—as the authority figure, no less—tasted like the bitterest of ironies.

But then I thought about it for awhile. I had been offered a chance to make a difference in the lives of potential young writers, to turn some of them from the path of academia—or, worse yet, technical business writing—and toward the great clearing of the mind called fiction. To encourage them to pursue their artistic selves, to dwell in a world where every eight-and-a-half by eleven piece of blank paper bursts with possibilities—this, I saw, was an honor. I could educate them about something that really mattered. So I called Darlene back and told her I'd do it.

That was the best moment of my teaching career—the glory I imagined before reality intruded and pissed all over me.

Darlene failed to tell me that I would never actually set foot in a classroom on the University of Southeast Arkansas campus. I had imagined myself coming home from a rough half-day of classes in which

I had nourished a kernel of idealistic characterization into something real and breathing, alabaster chalk dust staining my fingers, my bladder full from too much coffee and Coke, my stentorian voice hoarse from sprinkling praise and damnation amongst my students' dreams. But then I actually met with my new department head, a hornet named Maxine Bellafonte.

She was an endowed professor of English and Women's Studies and had published extensively on feminist issues in contemporary literature; in fact, I later discovered that she had written a long, scathing article on the female protagonist of my first novel. She thought I was a misogynist, though I didn't know that when I met her.

Wanting to make a good impression, I dressed up in a suit and tie, put on my best brown loafers, and gargled with enough Listerine to drown a pony. I tried not to smirk when I met her, even though she looked like a desiccated grasshopper. Her jet-black hair was pulled back in a matron's bun so tight that it threatened to split her face down the middle. In her dull gray business suit, she looked like Arkansas's creakiest funeral director. Her nose was sharper than the letter opener she was idly fingering, her pointy eyes narrowed and suspicious behind her librarian's glasses. Sitting across the desk from her, I felt as if I had wandered into a *Saturday Night Live* sketch about lesbians, ageism, and celebrities. No woman could be this stereotypical and live; yet there she sat.

I fidgeted while she shuffled through my application materials. Darlene had assured me that turning in some kind of resume was just a formality, since the Dean had already offered me the job, but Professor Bellafonte scrutinized my vita as if she had dropped her dick in my letters of reference. When she finally spoke, her voice sounded exactly as I had imagined: low, grating, and full of the bitterness only lonely old women can really understand. She said

Mr. Seymour, I'd like you to know that hiring you for this position was not my idea, nor do I agree that you should be given the opportunity to spread your brand of gender fuckery to our students

and, stunned, all I could think of to say in reply was

Did you just say gender fuckery?

and she said

Yes, Mr. Seymour, gender fuckery. I find your fiction rambling and narcissistic, your female characters little more than paper dolls that you dress and undress for your own satisfaction, your narrative voice the

112

intellectual equivalent of *Green Eggs and Ham*. I dislike your work so strongly that I nearly resigned in protest of your hiring and would have gone through with it, had I not seen it as my sacred duty to protect our budding writers from your contagion.

She glared at me as if she wanted to chomp my head off and swallow it whole. I was stunned. I had never seen this woman before in my life, and she had just eviscerated me. Worse, she had insulted my work. Since when was I required to advance the feminist movement in every piece I wrote? My face reddened; my heart triphammered in my chest. But I refused to give her the satisfaction of goading me into a counter-attack. If she planned to brand me an immature woman-hater, I refused to prove her point. So I said

Gosh, Mrs. Bellicosity, I don't know what to say. Have I made you angry?

She ground her teeth so hard and pressed her lips together so firmly that I thought her mouth would implode and suck the rest of her head in with it. One could only hope. But after a few seconds of tense silence, she said

My name, Mr. Seymour, is Professor Bella-fon-tay. And yes, every time you have put pen to paper, you have made me angry

and I said

Actually I usually write on my computer

and she snarled

That is not the point, sir. The point is that your work is anathema to me, and though I have no choice but to hire you, I don't have to let you set foot in one of my classrooms. You, sir, will teach English 7447—the distance learning course.

Not since Carol asked me if I'd ever consider getting a vasectomy had I heard words that inspired such horror.

But I resolved that Professor Tightass would not get the better of me. I would learn to use the computer system. I would teach the best damn correspondence class that ever existed. I would produce writers who would sell millions of copies, win Pulitzers and Bookers, contend for the Nobel. I would foster the early careers of future household names, just to spite that buzzing yellowjacket in the USA English department office. And online teaching would better suit my personality anyway. I've always been private, and as a writer, what I hate most is the book tour circuit—having to talk intimately to people I've never seen before. Professor Bellicosity had actually done me a favor.

I was drafting a syllabus when Carol came over for dinner that night. I had decided that each student would produce one story every three weeks; in the interim, we would workshop their stories online. Over a fifteen week semester, that would give each student a total of five stories— not enough for a collection, but a good start for them, and not so much burden on me. Carol, of course, took issue with all this. She said

Michael, you haven't workshopped anything since grad school. You hate the very idea of workshops. How do you know how to run a session like that?

and I said

It's not rocket science, honey. You make the students post a draft of a story. You give them some guidelines on how to be constructively critical. And then you push them toward the stronger advice

and she said

And what happens when they start sniping at each other like a bunch of kindergarteners?

and I said

Perhaps you didn't hear the part about guidelines for constructive criticism

and she said

Michael, have you ever met any writers? You people don't know how to be constructive when it comes to your competition. Or have you forgotten your review of Digby Darrymore's last novel?

and I said

That's different.

She had a point, though. I had savaged Digby's book, a preening doorstop about a college football player's stream-of-consciousness ramblings during the last fifteen seconds of a bowl game. Digby always takes a tiny moment of time and stretches it out over a thousand pages or more. He thinks he's James Joyce, but he reads more like James Fenimore Cooper on LSD. Even so, some critics love him. They think he's the great-est thing to hit postmodern American literature since Toni Morrison. What a crock of shit. He's impenetrable and twee. If that makes you a great writer, I can crank out a postmodern masterpiece the next time I have a 105 degree fever. So yes, I had ripped Digby's book apart, although I couldn't see what that had to do with my class. But then Carol said something that I put very little stock in at the time, though God knows I should know better by now. She said

And what happens when some star-struck little coed with big old cyber tits decides that she wants to meet the great Michael Seymour in real life and see if his sword is mightier than his pen?

I just snorted. After all, how dangerous could a star-struck coed be if all she had was an email address?

By mid-term I had been put on indefinite administrative leave pending the departmental investigation into the Hetty Irvington Affair. You might be able to understand my shock when the courts and the USA English department failed to dismiss Hetty's allegations. People crawled out of the woodwork to say I told you so—Dray and Carol, naturally, but also Morrie, and especially Professor Tightass.

But I'm getting ahead of myself, which I am wont to do when I'm feeling righteously indignant. Let me back up a couple of months to when classes began. I had long since posted my syllabus on coursecorrections.com, an educational site that served the entire USA population. Because I was teaching correspondence, I was required to use the site. Of course, this frightened Carol and Dray to no end, since I wasn't allowed online without supervision after my last shopping spree. But I swore on my love for Carol that I would do nothing but workshop stories, and since this job required an online presence, they finally had to trust me. I kept my promise, too. Never let it be said that Mike Seymour lies.

On the first day of classes, each of my new students sent me an email in which they told me a little about themselves and described what kind of writing most interested them—so-called literary work, genre fiction, screenwriting, and so forth. Two of my students liked high-falutin horkety-pork like Virginia Woolf and Gertrude Stein, those man-hating estrogen machines with inferiority complexes. The rest of my students wanted to be William Faulkner or Alice Walker or Stephen King. One email was so saturated with love for Tim O'Brien that I could almost see lubricant dripping out of my monitor. And of course everyone loved my work, or so they claimed. Mr. I-Love-Tim-O'Brien and Mr. Stephen-King-Rules were even savvy enough to critique Digby's novel. I knew I'd get along fine with those kids.

But Ms. Woolf and Ms. Stein worried me. They sounded, after all, like hardcore feminists. Those chicks always accuse me of writing flat, uninteresting female characters that fall into some stock category—the Wilting Flower, the Unapologetic Whore, the Virgin with Legs like Vicegrips. I think these critics ignore my stronger women characters, and they've never bothered to ask me why I write the way I do. Professor Tightass epitomized those prissy bitches, and I was just paranoid enough to wonder if she had planted Ms. Woolf and Ms. Stein in my section.

Ms. Stein's real name was Hetty—only a slight improvement over Gertrude, since both names invoke images of a ninety-five-year-old matron, not a twenty-six-year-old grad student with delusions of adequacy. Hetty wrote the longest getting-to-know-you email I received; it took me twenty minutes to finish. She detailed for me her earliest writing dreams, her weak attempts at imitating favorite artists, her discovery of high modernism and the history of Stein's salon, her admiration of how Stein mentored Hemingway and Anderson, and her aborted first novel about a woman who throws herself from a train and into a gorge, like something out of a Yosemite Sam cartoon. She included a full-body picture of herself, which in retrospect should have rung the first alarm bell. This picture revealed the world's only living debutante spinster—a pinched face with high cheekbones, hooked nose, thick bifocals, frizzy blondish-gray afro, an angular body that could have been cut from sheets of plywood, pale limbs jutting out of a checkered blouse and skirt. I kid you not when I tell you that this woman was the polar opposite of my type. I like curves, softness, body parts I can squeeze without cutting myself. Even if you doubt my professionalism, you shouldn't doubt that. A look at my dating history would exonerate me.

But Hetty Irvington knew nothing about my dating history or my preferences. She only knew my work, the part of me that one of her emails called

your particular penetration of human evanescence

whatever the hell that means. I had seen her kind before. She was a fan, not a writer. Her prose was ostentatious, the kind of drippy purple yammering that even the most hysterical romance novelist would reject as too over-the-top, pure *Castle of Otranto* sentences without the fun gothic trappings. I have no idea how she ever got a degree. I read most of her stories while taking a shit, and if she had ever found out, I don't think she would have had the sense to be offended. In short, Hetty Irvington was a lousy writer with a crush on the only published author she knew.

One day Hetty turned in a sixty-page story about a mortician's wife.

The subject matter disturbed the hell out of me; the main character couldn't sexually climax unless she stuffed a newly-arrived corpse's severed finger up her ass. Reading this tale in the john, I shuddered and let out a particularly sonorous fart, the two most appropriate reactions I could think of. I commented in the margins for as long as I could possibly stand it, about twenty pages, and then I skipped ahead to the summation. I wrote it longhand and typed it up later and attached it to the annotated copy. I provide it here in the interest of full disclosure.

Hetty,

I don't really know what to say about this story (and I use the term loosely) other than to suggest that you try again. Your main character is poorly drawn—is she a victim of her childhood trauma, or is she an active and self-aware sexual being?—and your narrative voice changes for no good reason at least fourteen times. The story is far too long for any reputable journal to publish, yet it's too short to be a novella. You also make a huge mistake in trying to cover her whole life. It's hard to do that in a novel, much less a story. Your sentences often tangle themselves around too many expletives and prepositional phrases, and your time order is so convoluted that it's impossible to know what happens when. In other words, everything that should make this story work is either absent or in dire, pressing need of revision. Maybe you should try your hand at a novel? But before taking your career any further, you might want to take ENGL 7835 (that's Forms of Fiction, in case you've lost your catalogue) and try to focus more on plot and characterization, less on deep and confusing philosophies. You aren't Kant, and you aren't writing his kind of text, so don't try to write like him.

MS

I sent the story back to her. I heard nothing more from Hetty Irvington for six weeks, not even when other assignments were due. I convinced myself that she had given up without dropping the class; I know from my own university experience that such things happen. Perhaps she had even quit writing, which might have been for the best. In any case, Hetty Irvington had faded from my life. Or so I thought.

I want you to look back at that note. Look at what I said to Hetty Irvington and what I didn't say. I could have told her never to write a single word again for as long as she lived. I was thinking it, but I didn't say it. Instead, I said try again

a much kinder phrase than the text deserved. I pointed out specific ways that the story failed as a story. Was I as careful with Hetty's feelings as I could have been? Probably not—I didn't offer any praise, but that's because I found nothing worth praising. What was I supposed to do, compliment her on her efficacious use of the spell checker? Congratulate her on remembering her own name? I certainly couldn't just make something up, though with Hetty's grasp of fiction, she probably wouldn't have noticed the difference. Sure, I didn't criticize her in the most New Age-y, touchy-feely way. I got right to the point. But I could have told her to piss off, to go jump off a bridge and stop taking up valuable oxygen. I said none of those things. I only suggested that her so-called story had been poorly conceived and badly executed. I didn't think she'd take my comments as the words of an angry god.

I guess some clichés have survived because they're true: you live and learn.

Six weeks after I sent the story back to Hetty Irvington, or approximately five weeks after I had forgotten that she existed, I heard a knock at my door around 6:30 on a Thursday night. I thought she was the pizza boy; I had ordered a large pie to tide me over through an evening of reality shows, gritty procedural dramas, and slow tinkering on a sestina. I had set up my TiVO, touched base with Carol, and unplugged the phones. I sat deep in thought, knowing that I only had thirty minutes to come up with another use of the word termagant. My mind reeling with possibilities, each lousier than the last, I opened my front door, twenty-dollar bill wadded in my fist, and said

Twenty-five minutes—you almost missed it, bu—

I was going to say buddy, but my voice trailed off, because the zit-faced pizza boy was not standing in the doorway; instead, I saw a tall, rail-thin woman in a ratty business outfit. She looked as if she hadn't changed clothes in a year. The skirt was frayed at the edges and soiled so much that I couldn't tell what its original color had been. It was polka-dotted with unspeakable substances. The blouse might have been white in another life, but it had been shredded to ribbons. It was gray in places, deep brown and black in others. She wore no shoes. Her unshaven legs, hairy as a caveman's, seemed oddly flattened in places; after a moment I realized that she was wearing torn panty hose. Her hair sprouted at odd angles and was caked with fragments of leaves, blades of grass, and multi-colored goo. And my God she was skinny, like she had eaten only by instinct and with no regard for what she put in her mouth. Her teeth had turned greenish-black. She smelled like a corpse rotting in an Arizona outhouse, odors of waste and decay wafting off of her in waves nearly visible.

I didn't recognize her. She looked like a hellish version of someone I used to know, the badly formed stick figure that chases you through a nightmare wearing the face of your best friend, blown up and stretched like a balloon. Her eyes were wide and hollow but not empty—fiery, as if her entire life had coalesced there. I said nothing to this apparition; I had no idea how to greet her. So we stood there regarding each other, my threshold's imaginary barrier separating us, until she spoke, her voice barely a whisper. She said

I'm not Kant

and then she fell on me, her hands around my throat, the stink of her breath wilting me like a flower in a blast furnace.

What happened after that seems anticlimactic. According to the physicians who testified at my hearings, Hetty Irvington weighed ninety-five pounds when she showed up at my house. She probably hadn't eaten a decent meal in weeks, and God only knows where she had been sleeping, or how much. Her attempt to strangle me probably represented the last of her flagging strength. She managed to topple me, and her ragged fingernails scratched me up pretty badly.

But getting her off of me wasn't hard. I just grabbed her wrists and pulled. One of them broke in my hands; I heard it snap like a rotting twig. She didn't even moan. I rolled her over and shoved her away and that was pretty much the end of it. She curled up in the fetal position and lay there, staring at the wall. I called 911 and asked for the police and an ambulance; Hetty Irvington never moved until they arrived. When the paramedics set her wrist and loaded her in the ambulance, she offered no resistance. I told them the whole story and explained my history with the perpetrator, assuming that would be the end of it. But stories never end that way, at least not the stories of my life. Hetty Irvington would be back, like a malnourished Terminator.

I was on a date with Carol when the cops arrested me. I was halfway done with a great New York Strip—medium well, sizzling in butter, encrusted with cracked black peppercorns, a potato with butter and chives on the side—when two uniforms walked into the restaurant and hauled me away, giving me the whole Miranda spiel. The charge sent shivers down my spine and shrunk my scrotum more effectively than a pitcher of ice water—assault and battery, the complaining witness one Hetty Irvington.

The broken wrist was nothing. The scratches on my neck and Hetty's appearance pretty much confirmed my version of the attack. Plus, who would you believe—the respected author or the nutjob stinking from her own waste? It helped, of course, that I was telling the truth and that Hetty Irvington had obviously gone crazy. Even the cops didn't really take her seriously; they tossed me a bunch of softball questions about my communications with Hetty and exactly what had happened. I just repeated the same story and offered to show them my emails. I left that day a free man, but by that time, everyone in southeast Arkansas knew I had been hauled in, and why.

Celebrity is a funny thing. People who like you will defend you to the death, even if you're found standing over dead bodies with a bloody knife in one hand and a signed confession in the other. But some people hate you just because you have more money than they do. They'll believe anything, no matter how outlandish. Hey, did you hear that Mike Seymour eats broiled monkey every morning? No, but I heard that he fathered a love child with Cameron Diaz and sold it to white slave traders in Marrakech. That's nothing; I heard that he's really an alien and that his books are encoded with some kind of mind-control symbols.

After I was released, both kinds of people came out in force. Letters to editors were written. Anchors both local and national discussed me on the evening news. My editor appeared on Larry King twice; my agent annoyed Bill O'Reilly. I made all the right public statements, which my lawyers carefully constructed, marking the only time I've ever been ghostwritten. All of this continued for weeks after Hetty Irvington's accusations had been discredited. No one believed that I had tried to hurt her, but everyone thought that I had stomped on her dreams, which sounded worse than any physical beating. Hell, even I would have felt sorry for her if my own life and reputation hadn't been on the line; the poor woman was obviously unbalanced. During the whole rigmarole, emotions roiled through me every second of the day—pity, anger, desperation, exhaustion. I hated Hetty Irvington; I wondered if I could do anything for her. I wanted to expose every neurosis that I noticed in her writing; I wanted the whole thing to be over. Mostly, I couldn't believe it all started with a lousy story and a freely given, honest opinion.

But Professor Tightass believed it. One day I checked my email and found a message from her. In its entirety, it read thusly:

My office, Monday morning, 8:30 AM.

Professor Bellafonte relieved me of my teaching duties. In tones of triumph and rage, she informed me that I'd never work in the University system again. I had to listen as my writing, my characters, and my themes were insulted yet again. I took it all patiently. All I said was

So what you appear to be saying is that I can't finish out the semester?

I was right on that point.

I thought about suing the university for breach of contract and wrongful termination, but Carol talked me out of it. Lying in bed one night, she said

You should just let it go, Michael. What have you really lost?

She was right. My reputation took a hit in the short term, but soon enough everyone forgot about the whole thing. Oh, I'd get an odd look from an old woman at a reading every now and then, but everything seemed mostly normal in no time. My old students wrote long emails detailing their contempt for my replacement, a writer who had published one slim, poorly received book. One student wrote

I always knew that Irvington chick was nuts. I mean, did you read those stories?

I couldn't really say anything for legal reasons, but I agreed. Hetty Irvington had been crazy before I ever met her. Nobody goes bonkers because of one letter. Do they? My comments weren't harsh enough to send anybody off the deep end. And yet there she went, right over the edge and splat, onto the rocks below. And there I stood, staring over the cliff. I didn't push her, but part of me will always wonder if I could have pulled her back.

House Arrest

Sometimes I can still feel the pressure on my ankle. I always figured the bracelet would be like those weights baseball players use on their bats as they wait on deck—donuts, I believe they're called. Not that I saw a lot of the bracelets; I never knew many people living under house arrest. But I did know a couple. One guy had committed tax evasion on a damn near biblical scale, but he was rich and white and straight, so nobody seemed that interested in sending him to jail. His lawyers managed to delay the trial for two years and then worked out a sweet plea in which he spent ten months in a minimum security prison, playing Parcheesi and nickel poker with money launderers and inside traders. He told me the only person of color he saw in that place was the black guy who delivered the sheets every Wednesday. Check this country's maximum-security hellholes and it's the other way around. That's a big part of what's wrong with America, if you ask me.

I also knew a woman who had committed vehicular manslaughter. She got mugged in Atlanta years ago. The perps beat her into a coma; when she awoke, she spent months learning to talk again. Even after her recovery, she was never really the same, and one day, stone cold sober, she drove her car off the road and into a 7-Eleven. She managed to miss the gas pumps and the soon-to-be witnesses who were standing beside them; she drove right between two parked cars flanking the only available empty space, zipping through it as neatly as a stunt driver. According to the wide-eyed teenagers who had been pumping unleaded into their rusting two-toned pieces of shit, she never even slowed down, must have been going forty or forty-five. She jumped the curb with a shower of sparks and a screeching noise that, had it happened anywhere else, would have signaled the end of her ride and her car too, but only a few feet separated her from the 7-Eleven's counters of Pepsi and motor oil and greasy potato chips in overpriced, understuffed bags. She obliterated the display window, glass bursting up and out over her windshield, the sound almost musical. She drove through the whole goddam store and didn't stop until she hit the opposite wall, where her car pinned a customer like a bug in a science exhibit, nearly cutting him in half. My acquaintance's license was taken away and she was given a year of house arrest, the penalty so limp because of her mental problem. I always wondered what the victim's family thought about that, if they were mad or disgusted or just sad that it had happened at all.

I didn't do anything so dramatic. I was sentenced to six months of house arrest following my conviction for breaking the Cuban trade embargo. Let me tell you, if you're ever at a book signing and some Latino you never met offers you a box of cigars for, and I quote, writing the novel that always made his mother laugh even when her gout was a real bitch, you turn the guy down and let him buy you a coffee instead.

Such is my luck, and if you don't believe it, hang around me and watch. Some people dive into a barrel of dead fish and pull out a diamond tiara. I dive into the same barrel and pull out a dead fish encrusted with shark shit and scales sharper than a Ginsu. That day at the reading, I opened the box as the Latino walked away. I never saw him again. But the next guys in line just happened to be government officials, one from the Department of the Interior and one from the Department of Commerce. And there I was, holding a box of Cubans.

Yeah, I got six months of house arrest for taking a box of cigars I didn't even want. I don't even smoke the damn things. And it's not like I smuggled in a baseball team or Elian Gonzales or Castro's mother. It was tobacco that somebody else dumped in my lap. Frankly, I hate cigars, their dead rat smell and the greasy way they feel in your hand. I tried telling the judge all this, but he was sick of seeing wealthy people walk out of his court scot-free because of high-priced lawyers and political favors. Hell, I see his point. I'm the first to admit that this system of ours is royally screwed. But cigars? Six months in the house, no theaters or restaurants or book signings or meetings with my agent Darlene or my editor Morrie in their Hamptons house, all for cigars that some jagoff dropped on my table. Who else could this possibly happen to?

At least it wasn't jail. I knew I'd never last ten minutes in a real prison. The guys in there have very little to lose and wouldn't think twice about caving in the skull of some smarty-pants writer who had fumbled his way into their territory, especially since my crime looked so wimpy compared to manslaughter and aggravated battery and worse. I'm no candy-ass, but I'm not a murderer either, and if you put me and a murderer in a corner with a couple of shivs, he's going to take me down every time. And the so-called country club prisons, though safer, would be no less boring and inconvenient. So when the judge told me I had to stay in my own house for one hundred and eighty days, I tried to count my blessings. And you can bet that Carol and Dray, respectively my girlfriend and best buddy, really lorded it over me after sentencing. Carol had always hated the fans' gifts. Once a sexy girl who looked barely old enough to vote brought me a box of sugar cookies, each adorned with a picture of her perky little boobs. Carol threw the box out of a moving car. My defense was that I accepted the box without even looking inside because I was cranking out autographs, and the fact that this excuse happened to be true affected Carol not one whit. Dray, on the other hand, had been waiting for something like this to happen so he could say I told you so. For years he had been swearing that one day I'd get stuck with something I couldn't walk away from, and he was right. He usually is, the bastard. So after the judge read me the Riot Act, Carol patted me on the shoulder and said

Well, baby, you got lucky twice. No jail time or fines, and you didn't take a bomb from a terrorist

while Dray said

I told you so, buddy.

I knew that the next six months would be filled with comments like these. I'll be damned if I can figure out why the two most important people in my life take such pleasure from my misfortune. Sociologists call that *schadenfreude*. If this were somebody else's story, Carol and Dray's collusion in my misery would probably symbolize my inability to commit. Or maybe it would foreshadow an affair, a plot to steal my assets. In a way, those stories would be far simpler than my actual life.

And this is the nature of memory. Sometimes I think I feel that extra weight on my ankle and my mind wanders down the back alleys of recollection; then all I can think of is the night I had to leave the house, when I drifted into the same stories that everybody tells, even me, tales entitled My Woman Done Me Wrong—the story of the night I became convinced that Carol and Dray really were sleeping together.

So there I was, stuck in the house. I could visit any room, but I could not go out into my yard or walk to the end of the driveway and check my mail. One day I opened my front door and stood in it breathing deeply, letting the scents of Arkansas spring fill my lungs; I just needed some fresh air. Unfortunately, approximately six pounds of pollen sailed up my nose and I fell into a great sneezing fit, my eyes watering and my throat burning. I felt myself losing balance and pitched forward into the yard, and as soon as I crossed the threshold, I heard the ankle alarm go off. I shouted

Oh shit

and turned, running back into the house as fast as I could. I dove for the phone, hoping I could get hold of someone and tell them what had happened. But I had no idea who to call. So I went back and sat in the doorway, waiting for the police.

Carol yelled at me for thirty solid minutes, even though it was an honest mistake. Dray snickered and shook his head. And they left together, thick as thieves. Separate cars, same direction. I didn't forget it.

Maybe it was the isolation, or the inability to swing over to the Monticello Starbucks for a latte sprinkled with cinnamon, or all that leisure time in which to picture them together. They always seemed to be pushing a common agenda with me—stay off the Internet, Mike. Buy less stuff, Mike. Let me borrow your credit card, Mike. Night after night I lay in bed—sometimes beside Carol, sometimes alone—and imagined how it might have happened. Perhaps they met at his place one night to discuss how to stop me from writing accusatory letters to government agencies. Maybe they went out for coffee or to FedEx my latest chapter to New York. It could have been a chance meeting. Or maybe Carol offered Dray a ride home after one of our beer-soaked movie nights. Hell, they could have run into each other at a gas station. Sooner or later, in towns the size of Parkview and Pinedale, you'll run into everybody. And as friendly as we've always been, it's not that much of a stretch to imagine them hanging out while I was stuck at home. After all, they would always know where I was.

Once I get something in my head, it's tough to let go. I needed to know for sure. I couldn't just ask them; they could easily lie. No, I needed physical evidence. So I concocted a convoluted scheme that was sure to expose them and demonstrate my brilliance.

First, I had to get everyone together under circumstances of my own design. To that end, I told Carol that I wanted to broil steaks, accompanied by a lot of wine and a night of DVDs on the big-screen TV. Carol loves movies even more than I do, and Dray is an unrepentant carnivore who never turns down a free Black Angus. So I knew that they would both accept. This is the way you have to think when you plan to deceive those closest to you—diabolically, preying on weaknesses mercilessly. Carol suspected nothing. She said

Sure, babe. I'll pick up the meat and some salad fixings, and Dray can bring the wine. Say around 6:30?

Do you see the significance of her response? I invited two people. She accepted for both and even decided what Dray would bring. Doesn't that sound like something one half of a couple would do? I congratulated myself on my first bitter victory—the knowledge that my plan could proceed, and the deepening suspicion that it was necessary.

I never called Dray, but he arrived at 6:20 with a half-dozen bottles of wine. Clearly they had spoken, perhaps even met. This wasn't enough to incriminate them—they were friends, after all, and I already knew they spent time together—but it seemed like a sign. I felt my anger rising like a gorge, and I wanted to spit it right in Dray's face and watch it drip down onto his shoes. Every time he spoke, I heard what he might have been saying to Carol in their most intimate moments—how they had laughed at me, pawed each other like animals, their passion destroying furniture and curtains and all the trust we had built over the years. I had no real proof that these people, my closest companions, had done anything at all; yet I believed it. And in my belief I wanted to kill them. I wanted to smash Dray's face. I hated him.

I've thought and thought about that day. I've searched my mind, my heart, and my soul. And I have decided to blame the confinement. Oh, sure, I'm naturally paranoid. Everybody knows that. But when my personality disorders combined with house arrest, everything escalated. The walls seemed to close in; the street leered at me through the window. I could see it winding around the corner and away, leading anywhere, everywhere, and knew that I couldn't set one single foot on it. I was stuck in the house, inside the box that the judge had built for me.

Meanwhile, Dray and Carol roamed free. He sat there in my kitchen that day, laying the bottles of wine carefully on their sides, and I imagined him stroking Carol's hip in bed, sweaty and exhausted. He told me some corny-ass joke about a duck and two farmers and a backhoe, but I didn't really listen. I just stared at him and wondered what his face would feel like under my shoes. It's hard to imagine that level of rage now. I'm not trying to justify it. I'm just telling you I felt it, as real as a punch to the gut.

Dray suspected nothing. He should have been able to read my feelings just by looking at me. It felt like I didn't blink once during that whole hellish evening, and most of the time I just kept right on staring at him. My muscles tensed; my fists clenched; my nails dug into the palms of my hands. Yet Dray kept on laughing and joking as if we were still twelve years old and camping out in his father's backyard. We even managed to get through an entire bottle of wine in the forty-five minutes between his arrival and Carol's.

She burst in the door, flushed and breathing heavily—probably because she was carrying a double armload of packages from Brookshire's, but it looked too much like post-sex exhaustion to me. Never mind that Dray had been with me for three quarters of an hour, by far long enough for any post-coital glow to fade; to me, it just confirmed that I was onto something. She dropped everything inside the door and said

Michael, I'm dying here. Can you help me with some of these?

and, gritting my teeth, I said

Sure, honey. And I'm sure Dray can help you with whatever else you need. Can't you, Dray?

He didn't answer because he was still standing in the living room, deeply involved in a ball game and his glass of wine. Carol gave me her normally cute nose-scrunched-up-and-brows-furrowed look connoting her simultaneous confusion over and dismissal of whatever your problem is. But on that night I didn't find it cute; it struck me as condescending. I despised it. I tell you honestly that I have never hit a woman and have punched very few guys in my life, but I wanted to slap that expression off her face. Her slamming the door that helped imprison me, her bringing in the niceties of domestic life packaged in irregular plastic bunches, her goddamned expression—I wanted to belt her. I didn't, but I wanted to. It was perhaps the most deeply assholish thing I never did.

As the night wore on, I broiled the steaks and baked some potatoes. A last meal for two condemned relationships. And the wine flowed like a deep red river. I wanted everybody good and drunk. For one thing, it would lower inhibitions, make them less likely to lie. For another, I'd have a ready-made excuse if I were wrong; drunk people say and do really stupid things all the time. So I ate my steak and drank glass after glass of wine, and I listened to a few more of Dray's stupid off-color jokes, and I slapped Carol's ass once or twice as she walked by me. I thought I did a pretty good job of acting normal, even though my every muscle was tensed fit to burst.

And then the final act of the night finally began, as we put away the dishes, threw out the empty bottles, and sat our stuffed, drunken selves down in front of my television. Carol brought more booze into the living room; Dray picked out some movies and stacked them up between our feet; and I sat beside him on the couch, boiling. What actually happened next still haunts us all to this day, though not for reasons you might suspect.

You see, thus far I've been describing the events of that evening as if I were confessing to some dastardly crime I once committed. You might have noted similarities to Poe's yarn about the old man with the weird eye and the stubbornly active heart, and with some justification; when I say I had murder on the brain, I'm not exaggerating. Well, not much, anyway—I didn't want to kill them, not really, or even cut them out of my life. But I wanted them to know that I knew what they were up to and that I wasn't going to take that kind of shit, not even from them. I planned to confront them, to yell and curse and shove Dray around, maybe even punch him. I planned to call Carol disgusting names and, in the pure fury of my righteous indignation, make her break down and beg my forgiveness. I intended to guilt-trip them into submission. No, I wasn't out for blood, but I did want my pound of flesh, and I was just waiting for the right moment to pounce.

And then it came. I sat nursing what might have been my thirtieth glass of wine, and Dray was walking across the living room to put in a new movie—maybe *The Big Lebowski* or *Dazed and Confused*—just as Carol came back from the bathroom. They walked right into each other, their heads going

bonk

like two coconuts cracking together. As if they had choreographed it, they both took two steps backward and fell back on their asses, eyes squinted closed, teeth clenched. Dray growled

Fuuuuck

and Carol said something that sounded like

rrrrrttttttaaaa

as they landed. In spite of myself, I leaned forward, concerned, nearly spilling my wine. They sat there for a few moments, taking in what had happened. And then they burst into laughter, high and almost hysterical, the kind of laugh that rises into silence, into painfully stretched lips and breathy

heh-heh-heh-heh

and Carol crawled over to Dray and put her right hand on his shoulder, and he put his right hand on hers, and then they embraced, a clumsy hug, holding each other chest to chest as they guffawed. Meanwhile, I sat on the couch like an idiot. Sure, it could have been innocent. You're stone drunk, you collide and crack skulls, you fall on your rear end, and as the pain and absurdity subside, you laugh about it with one of your closest and oldest friends. It could happen to anybody. But that night, stuck in my house and rolling drunk and paranoid, I saw the final proof I needed. They were pawing all over each other right there in my living room, right in front of me.

What I planned to do next—and given my state of mind, the term plan might be much too generous—was to jump to my feet and exclaim

Ah ha. I knew it, you bastard, you slut, you lying cheating miserable shits. I knew it. You thought you were fooling me, but I knew. Knew, I tell you. I knew it all along, and now you're going to pay.

The first part of the plan went pretty well. I jumped off the couch in one great leap, as if I had been sitting on an enormous cartoon spring. But I never made it to the maniacal laugh and the accusation. I had failed to account for one variable—the DVDs that Dray had stacked at our feet. When I say I jumped, I mean it literally. For a second, my entire body hung in the air, and Dray saw me in the corner of his eye. His head snapped around toward me, his eyes wide. Comically slow, as if in instant replay, he shouted

Noooooooooooooo

and perhaps it was the alcohol or my distorted memory playing tricks on me, but I'd swear he even sounded slow, the syllable stretching out and out, his voice uncharacteristically baritone. And as my feet dropped toward the floor and the first syllables of my grand speech died in my throat, I saw the movie cases. Then I landed on them.

My left heel came down on them; the plastic crunched, the sound like snapping bones, and then the pile avalanched under my weight. A few discs flew to the right; a couple shot to the left. But the top one skated straight off the pile and arrowed down toward the floor, with me following close behind. My toes hit first and bent painfully forward, like a ballet step gone horribly wrong; my right leg flew out sideways across the carpet, unsure of what to do with itself. I overbalanced in two directions at once.

Now I'm not exactly a couch potato. I work out a couple of times a week, so I'm still in halfway decent shape. But relatively few men can suddenly do a half-split without consequences, and I am not one of those men. So when my right leg skittered toward the wall, as if trying to get the hell away from whatever was about to happen to the rest of me, I felt something in my thigh pull and stretch and then snap. The pain was intense, like someone had shoved a lit torch in my leg.

Then my left knee buckled and crashed into the edge of my glass-top coffee table, ripping my trousers open and taking an inch of skin off my kneecap. The force tipped the coffee table toward me, hard. It fell over and crashed on its side just as my body was falling forward and down, so the edge of the coffee table caught me flush in the ribcage. Air exploded out of my lungs even as my knee and torso seemed to catch fire; simultaneously, my head whiplashed forward, my chin smashing into my chest, my teeth crunching together with my tongue caught between them.

I rolled off the coffee table as quickly as I could, every part of my body in agony. My leg was numb; I couldn't breathe; my ribs felt like someone was spreading them with a rusty circular saw; and my tongue was shooting lightning up my jawline. My mouth filled with blood. I couldn't spit—I had no air—so I opened my mouth and just let it fall all over the carpet. It made an abstract smiley face, like a Jackson Pollock re-imagined by Hannibal Lecter.

Nobody said anything when I crashed and burned, and I halfway expected them to laugh. Hell, I might have laughed at me if I had been them. But once I started spitting blood, Carol screamed. I wanted to scream too; I didn't know if the blood in my mouth was coming from my punctured tongue or a ruptured spleen or what. But I was in too much pain to do more than fall back against the couch and groan. Whatever I had planned for the evening, it was over now, and I was at their mercy.

Carol bent over me, asking me if I were all right. Even in my pain-soaked haze, I thought that was perhaps the stupidest question I had ever heard. When I didn't answer, she said

Get your car. We've got to get him to a hospital

and then Dray was standing beside her, his face ashen, his eyes as big as silver dollars, saying

I don't know, Carol...maybe we shouldn't move him? Let's call 911 and she said

We are not sitting here for forty-five minutes while those morons in Crossett and Monticello argue about who's closer. We are taking him to Drew ourselves, and we are doing it now.

When Dray didn't move out immediately, she jumped up and grabbed him by his shirt, shaking him and shouting

What are you waiting for? Get the goddam car.

She practically threw him toward the door, and that's when I was pretty sure that they weren't having an affair after all.

Dray drove like a madman while I lay in the backseat, doubled over and bleeding from the mouth, my head in Carol's lap. She stroked my hair and whispered silly, untrue blurbs of comfort, like

Don't worry, baby. It's all gonna be fine

the kind of thing you'd say to a three-year-old with a boo-boo on his elbow. I must have passed out a time or two, because at one point we were zooming down the highway and the next thing I remember, I was lying on a hospital gurney. Three nurses were leaning over me, poking me in places and asking me if it hurt, Carol snapping

Of course it hurts, you morons. Look at him.

I could see Dray sitting in a chair, elbows on his knees, ashen face in his hands. He looked sick. I closed my eyes and everything faded again ... until I woke up in my own hospital room. Carol stood over me, holding my hand. Other people were standing behind her, but I didn't recognize any of them. Carol said

Hey baby...you're going to be all right.

A man in ER scrubs stepped forward and said

Mister Seymour, I'm Doctor Rosenhump. Don't try to talk yet. Your tongue took quite a beating.

I don't remember much of what he told me—morphine was my best friend that day—but Carol gave me the gist of it later. I needed surgery on my groin. I had broken four ribs; two more were cracked. Luckily they hadn't punctured anything inside me. I had also bitten off—and likely swallowed—a piece of my tongue; the reason that Rosenhump didn't want me to talk was because my tongue had been patched with enough stitches to hold a mainsail together. It had swollen up to twice its normal size. It didn't help that I kept laughing at Rosenhump's name; if you've ever laughed with broken ribs, you know what I mean. Nothing's funny for long.

When he finished his spiel, Rosenhump said

And now I'm afraid these gentlemen have business with you. I'll be back to check on you later.

My drug- and pain-addled brain finally fired the right synapse, and I realized that those gentlemen weren't wearing hospital scrubs. They were wearing police uniforms. One of them, a middle-aged guy with a pot belly and a porn mustache, stepped forward and said

Michael Seymour, you are under arrest for violating the terms of your house arrest. You have the right to remain silent. You have the right to

but before he could finish, I closed my eyes again.

Dray got arrested, too, for driving while intoxicated. The judge agreed to strike the offense from his record since he didn't hurt anybody and had only done it to help me. He also let me off easy, since I had not left my house under my own power. But the judge felt that we should have just called 911 like everybody else, so Dray got stuck with 120 hours of community service. He worked it off on a highway litter crew, partnered with a guy who had been arrested for failing to pay child support. Carol took care of me until I could get around by myself. I never mentioned my suspicions or my scheme. But one thing I learned about house arrest: don't have your hammered-out-of-his-mind best friend drive you to the hospital after you tackle a coffee table. Things won't turn out too well for anybody.

Phone Tag

If I had to pick one invention to destroy forever, I'd choose the cell phone. God, they bug the hell out of me. I mean, I leave home to get away from annoying calls. Now damn near everybody takes what amounts to a tracking device with them. I just don't get it. And if you must, I mean absolutely must, carry a phone with you, does it have to play the same annoying pop songs that I never wanted to hear in the first place? Does it have to have Internet access? Can't we find enough porn on our home computers? And who, in the name of all that's holy, needs a camera phone? Who wants to look at a bunch of itty-bitty pictures in the middle of a conversation?

I hate cell phones in restaurants. Your mother should have told you not to talk with your mouth full. I hate cell phones in theaters. Why come to watch a movie with a bunch of strangers if you really just want to talk to your friends? Just go see them and save yourself nine bucks. And I really, really hate cell phones in cars. If I nearly get killed by one more moron with a phone glued to one ear, I may punch someone in the mouth.

Now, I admit I own a cell phone. But I view it as a convenience, not a necessity. I carry it in case my car breaks down, not because my friend Dray might possibly call to tell me about a sale on large eggs at Rudy's Market or just in case my girlfriend Carol might want to discuss how, oh my God, her sister just totally took her favorite sweater without, like, even asking. I carry it if I'm in the middle of negotiating film rights, since my agent might call with time-sensitive information. But even then, I usually set it to vibrate. If I annoy my fellow human beings when they are trying to drive down the road without being sideswiped, I do it unintentionally, not because I'm an inconsiderate jackass.

Sure, at times I've wished I had my cell phone with me. Once I got stuck out at Parrott Pond, a few miles from town, and I really could have used it. But I didn't have it, so I hiked all the way back to Parkview. Some of my acquaintances from town even drove by, waving like idiots, as if I were simply out for my morning constitutional. You'd think someone would have stopped just to check on me, but no. A phone would help in a case like that, assuming you can get a signal. For the most part, though, I'd just as soon never see another one. And don't even get me started on those goddam walkie-talkie jobs. I can see absolutely no reason for those to exist, and if you can, you're either smarter than I am or much more gullible.

I've got to admit, though, that since I'm basically a misanthrope at heart, I like my voicemail. People can say they got in touch with me without my actually having to speak with them. It's like the buddy you take to the bar; it makes all the annoying conversation while you get drunk and eat pretzels and watch the Astros with the sound off. And because I love voicemail so much, I use it liberally. Carol and I argue over why I never answer my cell, even when I'm carrying it. She said

Michael, I don't think you've ever actually answered your phone. Do you even know that you're on the line when you open it?

and I said

Yes, I happen to know that, smartass.

As it happens, I didn't know, but I wasn't about to tell her that.

Most of the time, voicemail is my friend. But it does have a drawback, known colloquially as phone tag.

Back in the old days, meaning approximately fifteen years ago, phone tag seemed fairly innocuous. Oh sure, it could bite you in the ass in an emergency. I mean, if you needed a kidney or somebody to bail you out of the Redneck County Jail's holding tank, getting a busy signal or a series of unanswered rings could be catastrophic. But the worst that ever happened to me in the days before voicemail? I had to call somebody back. It didn't exactly stack up beside waterboarding.

After answering machines became so popular and we could leave each other messages, the frustrations of missed connections were easily articulated and impossible to miss. Messages progressed from

Hey dude, it's me. I need to holler at you about that business deal we talked about last week. Give me a call, 'kay?

to

Hey man, it's me. I called earlier. I'm just checking. Thought maybe

my message didn't get through or something. Call me. It's important
    to
    Where are you? It's been two days. I know you must have gotten
those other messages, man. Look, it's just my life here, right? Call me
    to
    Fine. Fuck you, motherfucker. I hope you die.
    Answering machines intensified conflicts because we left messages
at the moment of our greatest emotional peaks, the deepest valleys. We
had no time for decompression, for re-thinking our words and tone. I
firmly believe that answering machines increased the divorce rate,
homicide statistics, and felony assaults. And cell phones made it all worse,
because the whole point of a cell is that you can carry it with you almost
anywhere. They took away the one excuse we had for not returning
calls—not being home. And people only believe you for so long when you
claim that the officers of the court or the doctors in the burn ward would
not allow you to turn on your cell. Sooner or later, you've gotta leave the
building.
    When you play phone tag, all the frustration is doubled, because
both parties are trying to call someone who won't answer. You both think
the other is at fault. You both boil and seethe, and sooner or later
somebody explodes. I know. I've been there.

    I had traveled to New Orleans for a book signing on the weekend of
Carol's thirty-ninth birthday. She was depressed because her biological
clock was sounding its alarm, or at least building up to it. I was depressed
because I had no time to goof off in the Quarter, even though my hotel sat
smack in the middle of it. I wasn't exactly suffering, though; I was staying
in the Maison Homme Blanc, with its feather four-posters and private
courtyard. I woke up in the morning and inhaled the aroma of fresh
blueberry croissants and breakfast tea. I read my complimentary paper
and lounged at my table in the courtyard, listening to the muffled voices
from the street and the previous evening's rain dripping from the trees. My
cell was packed away in my suitcase. I knew I should call Carol right away,
but for all I knew, she wasn't even up yet, and I didn't want to wake her on
one of the few days she might sleep in, birthday or not.
    Like I said, I'm not a jackass.
    After I showered and dressed, I dug my cell out, turned it on, and
waited for the annoying beeps and boops that would signal the presence

of somebody's message. But nothing happened. No one had called—not Carol, not my mother, not even my agent Darlene, who had set up the signing and was probably scared that I was planning to destroy her network of friends and acquaintances in the greater New Orleans area. So I turned the phone off again, stuck it in my pocket, and headed to the lobby, where I waited for the car. It arrived half an hour later. I was due at a bookstore located somewhere in the Central Business District, not too far away, but traffic in New Orleans generally slows you way down.

Sure enough, we hit a traffic jam on Royal. A delivery van sat on the street near one of the hotels, while a bunch of tourists' cars choked the garage. Trucks and cars and minivans sat waiting to be driven into the city or valeted to a nearby lot, clogging the hotel's breezeway like metal kudzu. So the delivery van sat on Royal, honking its horn in long braying blasts, while I languished in the car directly behind the van. I too let off some long braying blasts, curses and epithets that I invented on the spot.

An elderly gentleman driving a boat-length Cadillac walked out and tried to move his car, the one nearest the street—blocked from the front by the five driverless cars in front of him, blocked from the rear by the delivery van, my car, and the eight or ten tourist-driven gas-guzzlers lined up behind us. This poor old guy could only shrug his shoulders and mouth the word sorry, because really, what could he do? At this point, it would have taken a hotel fire or a convention of traffic cops to disentangle us, and neither of those events seemed likely. So, with some time to kill, I tried to call Carol.

Now remember that I was trying to be the good guy, to do the right thing. But I also felt pressured, like two strong hands were squeezing either side of my head. One signing won't make or break a writer with any kind of reputation, but you don't want people to think you're flaky, either. You don't want to be the Axl Rose of the novelist set—the guy who schedules an appearance and then doesn't show up. All this preyed on my mind as my call got dumped to Carol's voicemail. I patiently waited for the beep, and then I said

Hey baby, it's me. It's—Jesus, what time is it? Oh God, it's nearly 11:20. [Sound of car window rolling down] Hey pal. Nobody's gonna move those cars. Get that van out of our way. [Sound of the window rolling up] Sorry about that, honey. Anyway, I'm on my way to the signing—at least I will be if this stupid asshole in the delivery van will ever get the hell out of our way—and I just wanted to call and say ... uh oh, hold on a second.

This guy's yelling something at me. [Sound of window rolling down] What? You got something to say? [Muffled, angry voice...the words prick and assrag can be heard] Screw you, buddy. Come over here and say that. [Muffled shout] Yeah, and your mother too. What are you, stupid? You think everybody in that hotel is gonna run down and move their cars just because you say so? Get the fuck out of here. [Muffled shout] Oh yeah? Well, it takes one to know one. I—what? [Muffled voice] Well...yeah. As a matter of fact, I am Michael Seymour. [Muffled voice] Yeah, me too. I have to get there in like twenty minutes. [Muffled voice] Oh, you're a fan? Well I tell you what. If you can move this van, I can hook you up with

At this point, the voicemail cut me off. But given all that was happening, I still think that my first attempt could have gone much worse.

Thanks to a half-dozen autographs, the delivery driver finally moved his van, and the traffic snaked down Royal and out of the Quarter with my car at its head. My driver knew the city's rhythms; he managed to deposit me on the sidewalk in front of the bookstore before my deadline. But as soon as I stepped onto the concrete, the store manager appeared, grabbed my arm, and rushed me inside. Apparently the staff wanted to take pictures and get autographs. They requested

To my best buddy

or

To my number one reader, all the best, hope you have a great career in publishing

but I just used my standard autograph, which said

Best Wishes, M. Seymour.

By the time they let me go, the doors were opening, and I had no time to check my messages. My phone sat in my coat pocket, forgotten.

A radio call-in show appearance was scheduled for that evening, so I barely had time to wolf down an oyster po'boy before dashing into the studio and plopping down in front of the microphone, breathless and exhausted. Physically, I felt like I had run wind-sprints with the Saints all day. Mentally, I was nearly catatonic. I had slept poorly the night before and had spent the day talking, signing, glad-handing a bunch of people I would never see again, half of whom wouldn't remember what I said to them by next week. And still the radio show—an hour with a snarky host who always thought that he knew more about literature than the great

139

unwashed, and callers who proved him right. One caller said

So Mike

They always call me Mike, as if I'm their best friend and we're having a beer in our favorite pub

So Mike, your books seem to get more and more ambitious in scope, in other words longer, but I'm not sure that your themes have changed. What are you really trying to prove?

and I said

Well, I

and the host said

Oh please. In case you've just joined us, Fred from Metarie has just asked Mike Seymour what he's trying to prove in his books. Folks, Michael Seymour has won more awards than Gore Vidal and Robert Penn Warren combined

This wasn't true

and he's got more on his mind than proving something to you. If you look at the contemporary writer from a purely post-structuralist perspective, then you have to admit that

This went on for some time. Before the host was done, he had name-checked Hegel, hermeneutics, ontology, Derrida, and, somehow against all reason, Milton Berle. I knew his story. He was a grad-school dropout, a guy who dreamed of a university's hallowed halls, of engaging in deep and meaningful discussions with starry-eyed students. But he couldn't understand the theory or keep up with the workload or pass the dissertation defense, so he dropped out and took a job where he could talk about literature as much as he wanted and hang up on anybody who knew more than he did. I rolled my eyes at everything he said, but he paid no attention to me. I probably spoke for ten minutes, tops. And some of the callers didn't even care about the book, didn't seem to know me at all. One wanted to know if I were married to Jane Seymour, the actress. I said

Yes, as a matter of fact, I am. We vacation in Taiwan every year and pay the local girls to fistfight in a tub of butterscotch pudding

as the host made shushing noises at me. Another asked me about my favorite writers. I said

What, are you crazy? I don't read.

I played a different kind of phone tag with them. They pretended to have something to say; I feigned interest and made up answers. It was give and take, tit for tat, *quid pro quo* Clarice all the way. All I really wanted to do was get the hell out of there and call Carol. By this time, only a few hours of her birthday remained, and I had to get hold of her or risk sleeping alone for a month. And when the show finally ended, I ran out the studio door while the snarky host was still plugging my book.

I hit the sidewalk and looked for my car, but it was gone. I hoped the driver had just decided to circle the block. So while I waited, I tried to call Carol again. I figured she wouldn't pick up, but then I heard her say

Hello.

It's always a statement with her, never an interrogative. Hello. Like she's telling you it's her conversation, right from the get-go. She puts a lot of people off, but I'm used to it. So I said

Happy birthday, babe.

I waited for her response—the recognition, the warmth creeping into her voice, the connection between us bridging all the miles and the cell towers and the yellow taxicabs taking people to dinner and the bars and the houses. I waited, and I waited. Then she said

Hello.

Emphasis on the final syllable—curt, annoyed, her voice clipped and harsh, like a spatula on a frozen windshield. Louder this time, I said

Happy birthday, babe. It's me, Mike.

On her end, only silence. I tried again, but before I got past Happy, she interrupted and said

Look, I don't have time for this. If you're going to say something, say something.

Obviously we had a bad connection. I could hear her; she couldn't hear me. I could shout until I was blue in the face and my throat bled, but it wouldn't help. I said

Fuck

and hung up. I called her back again, but she had turfed her calls to voicemail. She must have been in the middle of something—cooking dinner, watching a favorite show, drinking her celebratory bottle of Pinot Noir all by herself. Briefly, my paranoia whispered dark things in my ear—she was mad at me, she had decided to leave me, she was seeing my best friend Dray behind my back and in no position to talk. I had had these suspicions before. But they had never brought me anything but trouble, so I tried to put them out of my mind. I left a message that said

Hey, babe, happy birthday. I've been thinking of you all damn day. I wish you were here, and I'm hoping you had a good time doing whatever it is you decided to do. Can't wait to hear all about it. Love you. Bye.

Of course, I could wait to hear all about it. I really needed some sleep. But you can't say that to your girlfriend, especially when you're traveling on her thirty-ninth birthday, when she's in southeast Arkansas hopefully alone and you're standing on a sidewalk in New Orleans, wondering if your car's coming back or if you need to ask the jackass DJ to call you a cab. You say Can't wait to hear all about it, love you and pretend you mean the first part because you really do mean the second part. You play the game that everybody plays and you hope for the best. And when your stupid car service abandons you before their job is done, you try not to take it out on the cabbie.

I called Dray to ask if he had seen Carol, but I really wanted to find out what he had bought her. We'd all known each other forever and the bastard always managed to get her better presents than I did. Plus, I was jealous, because I was traveling and he wasn't. I sat in a hotel room—a nice one with a great mini-bar paid for by some accountant, but a hotel room all the same. I drank little airplane bottles of hard liquor and ate expensive macadamia nuts out of cheap-looking packages and watched a ball game on ESPN. I tried calling Carol twice more before I fell asleep on the bed, on top of the covers with my clothes still on, the combination of alcohol and exhaustion too much for me.

At 11:30 I snapped awake like someone had thrown water in my face. I had been having a terrible, vivid dream, the kind where the colors seem to bleed out of your closed eyeballs like tears and the sounds seem so real you can practically feel their textures. I had been wandering down a New Orleans sidewalk, listening to the sound of a street-corner jazz band, the music drifting along with me like a light breeze. They were playing Celebration by Kool and the Gang—not exactly a jazz classic, but I definitely recognized the melody. The day was bright and sunny, the kind of sky that hurts your eyes even when you're not looking up, the sidewalks so bright it's like they've been sandblasted and polished. I strolled along until this homeless guy came out of nowhere and threw his arm around my neck like we were best pals. He hadn't shaved in years; squiggly things cantered about in his dirty beard. His teeth were black and his eyes dull, his breath blowing out of hell itself, and he said

When was the last time you heard a busy signal?

I threw him off and started running, sudden panic rising in my throat like bile, and as I ran the sky lost its luster and turned black, the clouds boiling over the tops of buildings, dropping lower with every step I took. But this was no storm, because the people I passed seemed unaware, their hair unruffled by the same wind that pounded against me and threatened to lift me off my feet. It was pushing me along toward something I couldn't see, a blurriness in the distance that was neither city nor horizon, more like a blank place in my imagination, the place where lost ideas crawled off to die, and as the wind pushed me harder and harder toward it, I realized that Celebration had transformed into the theme from *Jaws*, and every bass note brought me closer to whatever oblivion lay in the heart of that blankness. I tried to scream and the wind whipped the sound away, and as the music got faster and faster I finally yanked myself awake.

I sat there panting and stewing in my own sweat until I realized that I was hearing an intermittent beep, the kind that my cell phone makes when I have a message. Someone had called or texted and I had slept through it, and before I even looked, I knew who it would be. I dialed my voicemail and listened to the usual menu, waiting to assess the damage. And when Carol's message started to play, I knew from the first word that I would, as Ricky Ricardo used to say, have some splainin to do. In a tone that suggested sharpened rusty knives, Carol said

Hello, Michael. It's me. I guess I missed your calls earlier. Dray stopped by and we watched *The Notebook* together. It was his idea. He always knows what fits the mood, doesn't he? A movie about romance and heartbreak—perfect for a birthday I didn't want to have and a lover who isn't here. We drank a few toasts in your honor and Dray defended you every time I got pissed about you not calling me back. You must have had a good reason, he said, and I had to admit that you at least made the effort. That's an improvement over some years, isn't it? I guess we're making progress in spite of ourselves. I'm sorry if I'm coming off like a whiner. I don't mean to. It's just that this birthday has been tough on me. I thought I'd be married with a family by now and proving the great feminist credo, that you can have it all if you want it. Not that I'm pressuring you. It's just—oh shit, I don't know what it is. This isn't the message I meant to leave. I'm sorry for rambling, and you shouldn't feel guilty about anything. This is my deal, and I'm really pretty much okay. It was a decent day. Thanks for calling. Love you, and I'll see you when you get home. Bye.

I hung up, thinking that I had gotten off pretty easily. But as I tried to go back to sleep, my conscience kept jabbing me in the ass, making me turn over and stare at the ceiling. I really hadn't had a great reason for not calling her again. For the last few hours I had been sleeping in a terribly uncomfortable position and brewing up a good case of skunk breath, a mixture of closed mouth and bourbon and vodka and macadamia nuts. Hardly a crisis, right? I couldn't wait until morning to call her back. It was only 11:30. So I speed-dialed Carol and hoped for the best.

By the fourth ring, I knew that I was going to get her machine yet again. So I hung up and speed-dialed her cell. Again I imagined her snuggling up to Dray in our bed, her leg thrown over his, her hand on his chest. They were both naked and sweaty, his limp dick lying across his hip like a dead garden snake. I shook my head as hard as I could, my brain rattling against my skull with a swishing sound, and as the image dissipated, I heard Carol's goddam voicemail message. It said

Hello, I can't come to the phone right now. If you'd like me to call you back, leave a message after the tone or try me at Michael's numbers.

I've never understood why people say they can't come to the phone right now. I mean, the whole point of a goddam cell is to carry it with you. You might as well say that you don't feel like answering or that you're screening your calls to avoid telemarketers and relatives. But when the phone beeped at me, I did my duty and left the best message I could think of at the time. It said

Hey babe, it's me again. I guess we're just going to play phone tag all night. This last one is my fault. I made the mistake of sitting down on the bed to watch TV, and the next thing I knew, I woke up after eleven. Look, I'll make sure Darlene never schedules another appearance on your birthday again. And I'm glad Dray was there for you. I'll be home as soon as I can, and I'll make it up to you any way you want. Still love me? Because I love you. Bye babe, and again, happy birthday.

Not exactly Shakespeare, was it? Some of it sounded sappy, and in other parts, I lied; for instance, I was not glad Dray stopped in. I wished he would have stayed in his own goddam house and gotten his own goddam girlfriend. But I sure couldn't tell her that, or that I was still half-drunk and depressed and felt like I had worked road construction in Nevada all day. No, I had to use the old stand-bys, the same ones that have been failing couples for years, the I love you's and the I'm sorry's and the Whatever you need is fine with me's. Sitting in that hotel room in New Orleans, my bank account and reputation growing every time someone I'd never met bought my new book, my belly full of decent liquor and good food, I felt lonelier than I had in years. But I couldn't say any of that, either.

I lay back against the pillows and put the cell phone beside my head, even though I knew it wouldn't ring again all night. Whether she was with Dray or not, Carol would be in bed by now. She had to work the next day, and soon enough, she would have to pick me up from the Little Rock airport. I closed my eyes and listened to the beat of my own pulse, the rush of blood in my ears like the ringing of a phone, the absence of her voice like the disappointment of a lost connection.

Travel Plans

My mother once said that if I couldn't say something nice, then I shouldn't say anything at all. It's an old saying, but a good one. I've met a lot of people who deserve nothing more than a good cutdown, a biting remark, a well-timed *mal mot*. But often, you'll live a longer and easier life if you just keep your mouth shut. I'll give you an example. Once, my girlfriend Carol invented a new version of her world-famous casserole —something with mahi-mahi and a light coating of allspice. After she spooned some onto my plate, she tasted her own portion and said

This isn't as good as usual. Right?

Immediately I sensed my danger. I knew that if I said

Right

then she'd get mad because I didn't appreciate her effort. But if I assured her that it tasted just as good as always, she probably would have said

Oh, so it's always this bad, and you're just now being honest with me?

Since I was in a no-win situation, I pretended to be engrossed in the home improvement show on TV. She frowned and dropped the matter.

Thankfully, a great difference exists between slandering your girlfriend's cooking and lambasting a vacation, because this time, I just can't keep my mouth shut. People keep telling me that the Internet has slaked our thirst for easy communication and information. And I keep telling people that those goddam machines are after us. If they can't get us physically—yet—then they'll come after us emotionally. Not to sound too *Terminator* or *Matrix*, but the survival of the human race may depend on nothing more than our ability to log off and go take a nap in a hammock. And we'd better take that nap alone, because if the machines don't get us, we're damn sure going to kill each other.

It all started with the Beach Boys—not the '60s version with the great songs that will last forever, but the one that gave us Kokomo. Taking my mother's advice, I'll say the nicest thing I can think of—it's not my favorite song in the world. But some genius DJ at one of the Monroe radio stations played Kokomo one morning while Carol was driving to work. The lyric about Aruba got stuck in her head, and she decided that the only way to get it out was to visit Aruba as soon as possible. And at that point, my sanity began to unravel. Okay, I exaggerate. The problems didn't actually start until my best friend Dray—he who always butts in—talked me into booking the trip myself, using only my computer, a credit card, and the website prancearoundforpennies.com.

Dray found the website when he accidentally clicked on an ad for it. Most of the time when that happens, you instinctively close the new window, but for some reason—fate? God's hatred?—Dray decided to look around. Prancearoundforpennies.com promised to find airfare, car rentals, hotels, and tickets to attractions for only pennies on the dollar. He entered some sample destinations and was suitably impressed. He had been looking for a chance to drag me on a trip for God knows how long, so when he heard that Carol and I were going to Aruba, he invited himself along. He said

Look, Mike, you can't navigate worth shit, and Carol gets pissed every time you take a wrong turn. Do you really want to be responsible for driving her all over a Caribbean island you've never been to? Or for making her do all the driving?

and I said

It's not that I don't want you to go. It's just that we never get any time to ourselves. Besides, I can rent a car with GPS

but he said

Oh, so you want to hear that sickening computer voice telling you to turn left into a café or drive straight ahead off a pier? Give me a break. Listen, I'll bring Genndy along. We can relax by ourselves when we all need a break, and when we don't, you'll have two extra pairs of eyes to find the landmarks.

I knew he was right; he usually is, the bastard. Besides, Carol would want him along. I've known Dray all my life, but sometimes I think he's closer to Carol than to me. Case in point: he didn't care that I wanted some alone time with my girlfriend. He just wanted to make sure she had a good time. But what could I do? You can only be so paranoid about the people who are supposed to love you. Step over the line too many times and the guys with the butterfly nets come after you. So I gritted my teeth and said

Fine. I'll call the travel agent tomorrow.

But, as usual, Dray had a better idea. He said

What, and pay all that extra money? Let's just fire up your desktop and book it ourselves

but I said

Dray, I've got money. What the hell do I care about their commission? Let's let somebody else do the work.

But five minutes into the argument, Carol showed up and took Dray's side, as usual. She's always doing that. I've had to live with it because my ideas, outside of my books, never work. But I still hate it. When the two of them take over like they're the parents and I'm a juvenile delinquent who just needs the right boot camp, I tend to go off and sulk, leaving them alone to do whatever it is that they do. But not this time. I said

Fine. But if we're doing this, I want in on it. The last time I let you guys book a trip without me, I had to look at arts and crafts in Tennessee for a week.

So all three of us sat down at my desk and logged on to prance-aroundforpennics.com, the worst mistake I've made since I hired that pothead to install Carol's home security system. And the worst part? I saw it all coming.

Personally, I blame Dray. He recommended the site. He planned the trip. I had no say in the matter. I'm rarely even allowed online. I tend to buy too much junk I don't need, and then I get really paranoid about what the companies do with my credit card information. Hey, in this age of identity theft and fraud, you can't be too careful. So when we logged onto the site, Dray was driving, Carol was riding shotgun, and I was sitting in the back like the little kid who keeps having to pee. They huddled together in front of me, shoulder to shoulder, Dray's ass parked in my comfy office chair, Carol's in one of the straightbacks from the kitchen table. And I was standing up, craning my neck and shifting positions, trying to find a way to see around them. I had already become an afterthought.

Dray clicked on the package-deal option. We browsed through a few dozen sets; well, they did, anyway. I still couldn't see most of the screen.

They always do this to me. I mean, damn, I'm a best-selling, award-winning author who has touched the hearts of men and women alike. I said

Hey, how about scooting over a bit?

but Dray said

So what do you think? These first three packages are cheaper, but number seven looks more like what we want.

He was talking to Carol, not me. She said

Well, let's check out the others first. They might be better than they look.

So they spent twenty minutes clicking on the first six options, and from what I gathered, nothing seemed acceptable. The first three had good airfare prices and departure times, but the hotel ratings were sub-two stars. The next three had better hotels but departure times of six AM or earlier. If anybody had consulted me, I would have nixed all of those choices, because I hate getting up early and I can't stand fleabag hotels. But nobody asked me. They just huddled and muttered and nodded and clicked. After awhile, I left and ate a sandwich and watched *SportsCenter* while they canoodled. I mean, fuck it—if you aren't going to consult me, I'm not going to hang around and twiddle my thumbs.

They might have just been waiting for me to leave for all I know, because I had only been gone for fifteen minutes when they walked in the den, smiling and triumphant. I said

What? It's done?

and Carol said

Yep. We went with option seven after all. Mid-morning departure times, a four-star hotel for eight days and seven nights, and a four-door sedan for

and she quoted the price, enough to make a strong down payment on a Hummer, every cent of which I would be expected to pay just because I had more money than they did. I nearly choked on my Shiner Bock and sprayed some all over my coffee table. I said

Jesus Christ, you guys take away my credit cards and send me to my room without supper if I buy a hundred bucks' worth of DVDs, and now you blow high four figures without even asking? You ever think that this situation has gotten a bit ridiculous?

but Carol said

We used your AmEx. I know your credit limits. I pay your bills, don't I?

and I said

You write the checks and send them off, but the money comes from my account. And I would write the goddam checks myself if you two would get your goddam feet off my neck

and Dray said

Come off it, Mike. You wanted this vacation just as much as we do

but I countered

Actually, Carol wanted this vacation. I could have cared less. And you invited yourself

but they had already sat down on the couch, oblivious to my protests. It was go along with them or be left behind, and once again, I felt like a kid. I remember once when I was fourteen or so, my parents made me go on vacation with them to Branson, Missouri. I had a girlfriend and didn't want to leave her for a week, and I hated country music, so I protested and argued and kvetched. And in the end, I found myself sitting in a theater, listening to Glen Campbell and wishing I were dead. This vacation was taking on that same sense of inevitability. Carol picked up my clicker and changed the channel from *SportsCenter* to a rerun of *Designing Women*. She and Dray sat side by side and talked about the first things they wanted to do in Aruba, while I slumped in my easy chair and seethed, dark thoughts about pushing Dray off a fishing boat or pantsing Carol in the hotel lobby darting through my mind like flashes of heat lightning. As usual, neither of them paid me any mind.

I have yet to describe Dray's girlfriend Genndy, the fourth member of our party. She stood perhaps five feet, two inches tall and, I would estimate, weighed twenty-three pounds. Genndy was perhaps the skinniest woman I had ever seen outside of a famine prevention ad. If she turned sideways, she'd disappear completely. Her shoulder blades poked out of her back like vestigial wings, a sight that always revolted me, especially since she insisted on wearing tank tops and backless dresses. Her legs were broomsticks, her fingers long and sharp like a vampire's. I have no idea what Dray saw in her, and if you think I'm being shallow, let me tell you about her personality—like a bear trap with a bad case of herpes. She had a surprisingly deep voice, and she used it to complain about everything. I never once heard her say anything positive. When we met, she said

I've read two of your books, and I almost finished one of them.

That is literally the nicest thing she ever said to me.

Now I was going to be stuck with her for a week, and worse, I had to pay for it, which seems akin to writing a check for a thousand bucks to the first guy who kicks you in the balls. I once said

Dray, what the hell do you see in her?

and he said

She's a firecracker in bed

and, while trying not to gag, I said

I bet—smells like gunpowder, hurts your ears, and might just blow your nuts off if you don't run fast enough.

Dray was not amused.

So our day of departure arrived. Dray and Genndy showed up at 7:30 in the morning. He wore a light t-shirt and jeans; she had opted for a white tank top and Daisy Dukes. I swear I shuddered for five minutes. I tried to hide it, pretending that my coffee was too hot, but Genndy saw right through me. She said

What's your problem? You know you'd love a piece of this

and Carol, rounding the corner with something like fifteen hundred bags, said

Excuse me?

and looked at me like I had done something wrong, so I stammered

Whoa, whoa. I don't know what the hell she's talking about

and Genndy scowled and said

Oh please

and Carol threw a travel bag at me and said

That's great, Michael. That's just wonderful

and she stomped away, while I said

What the hell just happened?

Dray glared at both Genndy and me and said

Thanks, guys. What a great start to our trip. I'll go see about her

and he dropped his bags, pushing past me and into my bedroom without knocking. I could hear Carol's raised voice and Dray's calm one, but I couldn't make out the words. Genndy sat down on the couch and trimmed her toenails with her bare hands, literally ripping off the excess and dropping it on my carpet, where it protruded like punji sticks. I shuddered again, not bothering to hide it this time, and Genndy said

I ask you again. What is your problem?

and I said

152

Call me squeamish, but I've got no desire to jab your toenails through the soles of my goddam feet

and she said

Oh, don't be such a baby. God, you're hard to take

and I said

Well don't let me stop you from leaving, honey. I didn't ask you or Dray to come along. He invited himself, and as far as I'm concerned, you're nothing more than the leech that managed to attach itself to the underside of his balls

and she said

Oh that is so gross. And by the way, your new book sucks.

Before I could unleash a clever retort, Dray came out of the bedroom, looking serious and shaking his head at me. He said

Okay, here's the deal. She's still willing to go, but she needs some cool-down time. Bottom line, she won't ride with you to the airport. And she won't ride with me because that would leave you and Genndy alone. So Genndy's going with Carol and I'm riding with you.

This arrangement was not ideal.

For one thing, I was ready to kill Dray, not only for worming his way into my trip but also for positioning himself between me and Carol. I knew she wanted him along, so I was stuck with him, but I had counted on the two-and-a-half-hour drive to Little Rock as my own cool-down time. How was I supposed to calm down when the jackass was sitting beside me? And Genndy's very presence offended me. She had been in the house for all of ten seconds when she got me in trouble; what could she accomplish in two and a half hours? But in the end, what choice did I have? I could either put up with it and risk my sanity or say no and be labeled the bad guy again.

Carol refused to come out of the bedroom unless I left first, so Dray and I climbed into my Mustang and waited. Genndy followed us and hopped into the driver's seat of Dray's Kia Rio. And moments later, Carol left the house, locked the front door, and breezed past the car without even glancing at us.

Three hours later, we checked our luggage in the Little Rock airport. The drive had gone smoothly in spite of my trepidation; Dray and I talked sparingly about the Razorbacks, the Travelers, and the St. Louis Cardinals when we bothered to speak at all. Once he tried to say something about Carol, but I said

I don't want to talk about her with you anymore

and he shut up. I had finally had enough, and he had sense enough to see it, which meant that our friendship was still salvageable. If he had pushed me, I might have thrown him from the moving car and out of my life. I was that annoyed.

Now only forty yards or so from our gate, we lined up for the metal detectors. My laptop sat on top of its bag, heading down the conveyor belt. My shoes and watch trundled along right behind them. Ahead of me, Dray and Carol had already cleared the line. Behind me, Genndy unloaded object after object from her pockets—keys and change purse and God knows what else. I didn't know where it had all come from; her Daisy Dukes had very little pocket room in the first place. And as she took forever, I realized how badly I wanted to get rid of her. I rushed up to Dray and Carol as they put their shoes back on and said

You know, if we hurry, we can ditch her here.

I tried to sound sarcastic, as if I didn't really mean it. That way, if they both really wanted her to come, I could claim that I had just been playing around. At first, I didn't really know how to read the situation. Dray and Carol looked at each other, then at me as I struggled into my shoes, and then at each other again. Something seemed to be passing between them. And then Carol said

It would never work. Our plane doesn't leave for another hour and a half. She'll never take that long.

A light breeze could have knocked me over. I never expected them to consider the idea. But now that they had, I planned to follow through. I said

Leave that to me.

Dray didn't protest.

So maybe I took it too far. But I ask you, how far would you go to avoid vacationing with somebody you hated? Think about it. You wake up in the morning and hear her nails-on-a-chalkboard voice emanating from the next bedroom—possibly berating your best friend, or worse, moaning in the throes of passion. You go out to eat and she sits across from you, nibbling the salad cracker that she ordered and glaring at you because your steak smells good. You go swimming and you have to look at her body, a paper Halloween skeleton dressed in two postage stamps. You try to go to bed at night and can't get in the bathroom for half an hour, and when she comes out, she doesn't even apologize for using all the toilet paper. What kind of vacation would that be?

No, I couldn't stand the thought of it. So I didn't exactly think the plan through. I just went for it, full steam ahead, and prayed for the best.

I told Carol and Dray to go on ahead, wishing that I could get rid of him, too, knowing that Carol would balk. They grabbed their bags and ducked into the first restaurant they saw, a steak and burgers place on the right. I waited for Genndy, intending to take her to the bar located on our left. The plan was to get her drunk, ditch her, and board the plane while she sat in a stupor, wondering where we went—not the most brilliant scheme ever concocted, I know, but hey, I was pressed for time.

Moments after Dray and Carol disappeared into the restaurant, Genndy walked up, dragging her bag behind her. She looked around and said

So where are they?

and I said

They wanted to find a gift shop and grab some extra sunscreen. They said they'd meet us in that bar over there

and Genndy said

Okay, whatever.

She let me lead her into the bar. I selected a table in the back corner, hoping that she wouldn't be able to see Carol and Dray when they left the restaurant. Genndy sat down and pulled her carryon under the table. A waiter appeared and Genndy said

Whiskey and Coke

and I said

Wine cooler, please.

Genndy raised her eyebrows, but I ignored her. I hate wine coolers, but I needed to stay sober. We sat there in uncomfortable silence for a million years or so until the waiter brought our drinks. I took a sip of my wine cooler. Genndy drained half of her whiskey and Coke in one swallow and said

You drink like a fourteen-year-old girl

and I said

Yeah, and you're built like one. What say we don't talk?

She laughed and drank the rest of her whiskey and Coke and rattled her glass at the waiter. He appeared with another one. She sipped this one, and I cursed my luck. I said

What? Decided that you can't handle your liquor either?

and she said

I thought you didn't want to talk.

I checked my watch. We had managed to kill only ten minutes. It had felt like an hour of long, drawn-out torture. I had to up the ante somehow. So I said

This is boring. Let's play quarters

and she said

I hate that game

and I said

Yeah, but you hate everything. Come on, unless you're chicken.

It was a schoolyard thing to say, hardly befitting an author of my stature or, you know, an adult. But it worked. She glared at me and said

Fine.

We asked for a shot glass and a bottle of whiskey. The waiter shrugged and brought them to us. I slammed the shot glass on the table, filled it with whiskey, and said

Want to go first?

She took the quarter and pulled the shot glass closer to her. She studied the table for a moment, calculating force, angle, the possible deflecting properties of crumbs and watermarks. Then she slammed the quarter on the table. It bounced up, clanged off the glass's rim, and rattled to a stop near me. I said

Ooooooo. Swing and a miss

and she said

Chance.

I slid the quarter back to her and she took it again, calculated again, slammed it down. This time it hit low on the glass, not even close. I said

Tough titty. Drink up.

She raised the shot glass and downed the whiskey. She shuddered a little, her heavy-lidded eyes fluttering. Then she gathered herself and pushed the quarter back to me, saying

Your turn.

I refilled the glass and took the quarter. I had neglected to tell Genndy that I am a quarters champion. I have put Dray and Carol under the table a million times. I once won a tournament in New Orleans in which I outplayed fifteen other people in two nights. I am the Grand

Champion Poobah of Quarters, a fact that Genndy seemed to realize after I had hit my sixth straight bounce and made two rules: no touching a moving quarter, and no saying the word quarter. She had to drink three more shots because the moving quarter touched her twice and, after the second time, she shouted

Goddammit stupid fuckin quarter

which brought the waiter over, asking her to keep it down. I smiled at him and shrugged, whispering

She's always like this. Confidentially, I think she needs to get some help. You might want to alert security.

The waiter didn't ask me to stop giving her drinks, though. On my next shot, I missed and decided not to chance it. Of course, she tried to goad me right away, saying

No chansh? You pushy

and I said

That's right, baby. I'm a pussy. Here's the quarter.

She took it and shook it at me, saying

Don't you call me baby. I always knew you wanted me, but I'm with ... with ...

and I said

Dray?

and she said

Yesh. Dray. I'm with Dray. So don't you go getting any ideash. You won't be getting in theesh pantsh

and I said

I'll try to contain my disappointment. You going to drink that shot or not?

and she said

But I haven't bounshed yet

and I said

Yes you did. You missed. Remember?

Her brow furrowed. The whiskey was hitting her hard; she had drunk nine shots, not to mention her original whiskey and Cokes. After a moment she shrugged and drained the shotglass again. I refilled it and took the quarter, hitting my first shot. She frowned and knocked the shot back, dropping the glass on the table. I took the quarter, refilled the glass, and bounced the quarter back into it. She whimpered. I would have felt sorry for anyone else, but as far as I was concerned, this gorgon was getting what she deserved. Any minute now she would pass out or worse, and I would be able to saunter down to the gate and join Carol and Dray. Twenty minutes till boarding. The glass was still full, so I said

Drink up, Genndy. And since you just touched a moving quarter, you'll have to take another one.

She gave me the finger and picked up the shot glass. She studied the liquor for a moment. The quarter still lay at the bottom of the glass, though she did not appear to notice this discrepancy. Finally she downed the whiskey, though some of it ran out the corners of her mouth. She coughed and sputtered a bit. Her eyes had turned glassy and I leaned forward, expectant, waiting for her to fall over. She looked up at me, a plea in her eyes.

And then she projectile vomited all over me.

It spewed from her mouth like water from a firehose, straight whiskey and a little Coke and half-digested breakfast and stomach acid and bile. It hit me in the face, stinging my eyes. A bit dribbled into my mouth, and before I knew what was happening, I blew chunks all over the table. Around us, people cried out, jumped away, yanked their bags off the floor. The remains of my breakfast covered Genndy's carryon. Second-hand whiskey soaked my shirt. Genndy's face was streaked with tears; mascara ran down her cheeks. I was afraid to consider what my face looked like. And somewhere nearby, the waiter called out

Security. Security.

Understanding seemed to dawn on Genndy's face as the guards rushed over. She said

You did thish on purposh, Michael Sheymour. You fuckin got me drunk on purposh. You made me throw up. You shon of a bish

and I snarled

You puked on me. You puked in my mouth.

And then the guards appeared, hauling Genndy out of her chair, pulling her toward the concourse. She slurred

You shon of a bish. You did thish to me. Guysh—come on, guysh—itsh all hish fault.

I was still trying to wring vomit out of my shirt. I looked up at the remaining guards, a sheepish grin on my face. I said

Can you believe that? Some folks just can't hold their liquor. She ruined my shirt.

And then they grabbed me and dragged me out of the bar, each with a deathgrip on one of my arms. They could have been Teamsters; my toes scraped the ground as they carried me out. I shouted

Hey, what the hell? What is this?

and one of the guards said

You want to keep your voice down, sir. You're already in trouble for creating a disturbance in an airport

and I said

Wait now. I didn't create anything. It was her. She got drunk and puked all over me, even in my mouth. All I did was throw up after I had been thrown up on. Is that a crime?

They didn't answer. They just kept dragging me along like a rag doll. I craned my neck around, frantic, desperate for help. And as I twisted, I caught sight of Carol and Dray coming out of the restaurant, watching in horror as I was carted away. I managed to twist around in the guards' grip until I could see them better, calling

Carol? Dray? You've got to help me. They're arresting me because Genndy puked on me. Come tell these lunkheads who I am.

Carol glared at me and shook her head. The guards had stopped; they were watching her, probably wondering what would happen. She picked up her bag and glanced back at the gate, and when she looked back at me, I saw tears in her eyes. I reached out toward her.

And then she turned around and walked toward the gate. Dray looked from me to her and back again. Then he shrugged and followed her. I whined

No. Nooooo. Come back. Carol. Baby, please. And Dray, you bastard, she's my girlfriend. You come back here.

But one of the guards said

Okay, Casanova, that's enough. Come on now

and they dragged me away, kicking and screaming and calling for Carol.

Hours later, I sat in the drunk tank with Genndy, who was sobering up. Her eyes were blood red and puffy. One of the straps on her blouse had slipped off her shoulder; I could see a tiny wedge of A-cup peeking out from the neckline. After a while she stood up and came over to sit by me. She put a skeletal hand on my upper thigh and said

You know they left without us. And you know what they're doing in that hotel room. When we get out of here, let's go back to your place and get back at them.

Dried vomit clung to her stringy hair. Spider-web blossoms of burst veins colored her cheeks. An enormous pimple winked at me from just under her hairline. Her hand moved up to my crotch and began stroking it, and I said

This is the worst vacation ever.

Lights, Action

The tripod stood in the corner, the camera mounted on top. It was the newest model, with a bazillion megapixels and a super-sized memory card that lasted something like a thousand years. The lens cap still on, the camera sat there like an oddly designed coat rack, dormant and gleaming in the low lamplight, radiating an aura of menace and unpleasant possibility. Like the raven on the pallid bust of Pallas, it came to mean a great deal, not so much for its own sake, but because of what it showed me about myself. I'll do my best to be honest about what happened, but I may have to gloss over certain details that I just can't bear to share. Stories are like that, right? You never get the whole truth. You get an outright lie, a fabrication, at best a version of the truth filtered through somebody's agenda. The one who tells the best story survives in the reader's memory. It's narrative Darwinism. But I digress.

I had wanted a fancy digital video camera for years, but my girlfriend Carol would never let me buy one. Too unnecessary, she might say, or too expensive for something we'd use twice a year. I'd argue that it was my cash to waste, that I had too much money anyway, but it never worked. Every time I brought up a camera, Carol changed the subject. In hindsight, I think that she was afraid I'd pester her without mercy or consideration until she agreed to let me film us having sex.

My intentions were mostly honorable. I wanted a camera for a lot of reasons: to record everything in my house for the insurance company. To preserve the moments of our lives that we would want to remember when we were old, barbecues with my best friend Dray and poker nights with my agent Darlene and her husband Morrie. To film our kids, if we ever had any, when they played ball and opened Christmas presents and whatever else kids do. And sure, the possibility of homemade porn always lurked in the back of my mind. But I'm hardly alone in that regard. You can't tell me most guys really think about sitting at their kid's ball game with a goddam viewfinder fused to one eye. You want to make your own movies—figure the angle, adjust the lighting, zoom in. You want to star, too. That way you can watch it when you're older and remember when you felt like a stud.

Carol always invented excuses or just flat out refused. Still, those who know me will tell you that I am a persistent man. And so I demanded and hinted and pleaded and cajoled. If I made an unsuccessful sortie, I waited a few weeks before broaching the subject again. And then I'd casually mention that I wished we had a video camera for fill in the blank with innocuous bullshit. If she rejected an idea, I just tried something else next time. I probed and retreated and probed and retreated, seeking an opening or an unguarded flank, and I never, ever mentioned sex in the same conversation. You can call me manipulative if you want, but relationships are like a game of high-stakes blackjack: if you want to beat the house, you have to know when to hit and when to stay. And if you don't like the war metaphor or the card-game simile, come up with your own comparison, but for Christ's sake be honest and admit it's true. We all know that Joey Tribbiani was right: there's no such thing as altruism. You get what you can whenever you can or you end up with nothing. So yes, I wanted to shoot my own porn, but I also wanted the camera for the usual wholesome reasons, and I chose to emphasize the vanilla stuff. That's not a lie; it's simply a matter of focus.

One day I finally wore her down. I don't know if she finally bought what I was selling or if she just plain got sick of hearing about it, but she finally agreed to let me buy a camera and to keep her mouth shut about it. Two minutes later I was browsing through online retail sites. When I found the one I wanted, I one-clicked it and chose the two-day shipping option before Carol could change her mind.

It arrived almost exactly forty-eight hours later. The box, which was three or four times bigger than the camera, came packed to the brim with Styrofoam and software and cords. I extricated the camera from its nest and threw the manual to the side, ready to record every moment of the new day, from my BLT lunch to Carol's choice of sleepwear. But when I turned it on, nothing happened, and then I remembered how these things work; you always have to charge them for ten years or so before you can actually shoot anything. Sometimes I think the electronic age might be defined as instant gratification delayed by dead batteries and bug-filled operating systems. Sighing heavily, I fished the manual out from behind the couch and figured out how to charge the camera, which would, sure enough, take at least twenty-four hours. Luckily I had a story to work on; I had to disentangle my main character from her relationship with the selfish bastard who kept mucking up her life. I sat down at my desk and wrote for two hours, casting the occasional glance at the camera. Its battery light remained red.

That night, I moved the camera to my bedroom, plugging it in to the outlet in the corner. I was reading Digby Darrymore's new essay collection, *Paper Clips I Have Unbent.* Like most of Digby's work, every essay positively dripped with pretentious verbosity. He had included an essay about the time we took a fishing trip to Spain, and his description of the countryside—hillsides that rolled like the bowling balls of the gods, décor that sizzled in the tortilla warmer of the mind, that kind of shit—was giving me gas. I was preparing to write a nasty letter to the critic who called the book

The best contribution to American nonfiction this year

when Carol walked out of the master bath, naked from the waist up, wearing only a pair of black panties. Her heavy breasts swung with the rhythm of her steps, and I would like to describe her legs for you, but my gaze never made it that far down. I cast Digby Darrymore and the quote water the color and shimmering beauty of Tiffany lamps unquote onto the floor and pulled the covers up to my chest. I said

I never get tired of seeing you come out of my bathroom like that

and she smiled, perhaps even blushed a little, though it was hard to tell in the brownish light of the 25-watt bulbs she always made me buy. That smile implied that I had said something right for once, and I was hoping that it might get me laid. Carol crawled onto the bed, balancing on her hands and one knee, the other leg still trailing on the floor. She leaned over toward me, her hair falling on my face, her nipples erect, when she happened to glance toward the corner. And then she sat up, pulling the covers off me and over her own bare chest, shouting

What the hell is that doing in the bedroom?

I sighed and sat up, wishing that I had still been holding Digby's book. It would have allowed me to rip it in half dramatically while I said

Well, that sure was fun.

Instead, I just shrugged and said

It's charging. I wanted to keep it in here in case the light turns green before we're asleep. I'm itching to try it out

and she said

Michael, the manual said that it would take twenty-four hours. You know damn well that the light won't turn green tonight. I think you brought it in here because you want me to get used to having it in the corner

and I said

Huh? What are you talking about?

and she said

You want me to get used to it so I won't even really look at it after a while, the way that I don't really notice the dresser anymore. And one day you'll just happen to turn it on before we have sex, and the next thing I know the goddam video will be all over the Internet and we'll be the next Pamela and Tommy

and I said

Jesus Christ. Everybody knows that Kim and Ray J. were the next Pam and Tommy.

She didn't laugh, so I said

You really think I'm a shit, don't you?

and she said

I think you think of yourself most of the time

and I said

Christ, Carol, it's right there. It's not like I've hidden it in the air conditioning vent. You can see it. It's not on. I won't turn it on in here without your signed and notarized affidavit in hand. Okay?

She looked at me for a few moments, searching my face for all the tells that she's learned over the years—looking to the left too much, scratching my nose in the middle of a sentence, using more than one Um. She found nothing. And that's because I was telling the truth. I hadn't had any agenda when I moved the camera in the bedroom, no long-range dastardly plan that would leave me twirling my mustache and going mwah-ha-ha-ha-ha. I just wanted to play with my new toy. And so, finding nothing that raised any alarms, Carol lay down, turned away from me, and pulled the covers up to her neck. She didn't even say good-night. And just to be stubborn and show her that I was mad too, I picked up Digby's crummy book and forced myself to finish the essay.

Carol's fit only strengthened my resolve to use the camera however I wanted, but she was crafty. If we stayed at her house, she managed to get me out of mine without the camera. When we stayed at my place, she'd throw a shirt or a blanket over it. If I even walked near that corner, she'd say

What are you doing, Michael?

and I'd have to pretend that I was examining a stain on the blanket. Once I yanked off the shirt she'd thrown over the camera and left it lying on the floor, just to see what would happen. As soon as she walked in the room, she made a beeline for the corner and threw the shirt back over the tripod. And dammit, I had been using the camera, going through all the boring-ass motions of responsible adulthood. I had made the insurance video. I shot a game of H-O-R-S-E that Dray and I played in my driveway. I even filmed Carol as she came home after work. She smiled and giggled and told me to stop, all the usual crap that people do when you point a video camera at them. She didn't care about any of that. No make-up? No big deal. No bra? Eh. But once I brought the camera in the bedroom and set it on the tripod, she turned into Jonathan Edwards, all hellfire and brimstone.

It was time for more drastic measures.

One day before Carol came home, I plugged in the camera and secured it on the tripod. I got behind it and adjusted for just the right angle. I turned down the covers and spread rose petals all over the bed—cliché, I know, but a nice visual. And then I fixed dinner for Carol, all of her favorite dishes: chicken with feta sauce, Greek green beans, home-made bread with real butter, strawberry cheesecake for dessert. And wine—lots and lots of expensive, potent wine. Ass-kissing and alcohol—a powerful combination, and one that had worked many times, for better men than me.

Carol smelled a rat, of course. She wasn't dumb. As soon as she came through the door, she noted the absence of take-out and hollered

What are you up to, Michael? What did you do this time?

and I said

What? Can't a man cook dinner for his one and only without being accused of—whatever you're accusing me of?

and, coming into the kitchen, she said

The last time you cooked dinner for me, you had clogged my toilet and flooded my whole house with raw sewage

and I said

Well, you don't smell any sewage, do you?

Before she could reply, she spotted the chicken and beans. She grinned and sat down, saying

No, I don't. Thank you for this, Michael. These are my favorite dishes, and I know you hate to cook.

Then something funny happened; I started to feel like a jerk. I did only cook dinner for her when I wanted something. I had not only proven her right about me, but I had also managed to fool her into thinking she was wrong. But hey, if you're going to be a jerk, you might as well go the whole hog. So I poured Carol a glass of wine the approximate size of my leg and sat down across from her. I had set the table restaurant-style—white tablecloth that reached just above our knees, plates the size of hubcaps, silverware laid out as if we were eating a seven-course meal, cloth napkins dry-cleaned and pressed and folded as best I could. Instead of wine glasses, though, I had broken out our margarita set, so that Carol and I were drinking approximately six gallons of wine with every refill. When she saw the glasses, she raised her eyebrows and looked at me, but I pretended not to see, and she never said anything. I guess she had decided to give me the benefit of the doubt.

I should have stopped right there. Once I realized that she actually meant to trust me, to let the evening play out as I had planned it, I should have poured the wine down the sink. We could have enjoyed the chicken, which wasn't half bad, and watched a movie together on the flat-screen. I had a chance to change things, to duck back to the bedroom and turn off the camera and get on with our lives. Those kinds of moments have usually come and gone long before we recognize them for what they are—the pivotal episodes when we irrevocably determine the course of our destinies —the simple-sounding decisions when we write our fates in stone and try to live with the choices we've made. I should have paid more attention. But I told myself that the plan was going well, and if she looked a bit sad—if her eyes were too moist, her eyebrows raised until they wrinkled her forehead—well, it wasn't the first time, right? It was like she wanted me to stop myself, even though she had determined not to ask. It was up to me. I could have done almost anything. My choice? I poured her another glass of wine. She nodded her head, the movement almost imperceptible, as if she had come to some decision. I guess that made two of us.

The wreckage of the meal lay before us—a few beans that nobody wanted, a bit of fat that I had neglected to trim off a piece of chicken, some congealing feta sauce the color and consistency of hangover bile. Two bottles of wine lay empty on the kitchen counter; another half-full one stood upright on the table. Carol's glass was empty again. Her head lolled from side to side, her eyes unfocused and hazy. They kept trying to close and she kept snapping them back open. But the corners of her mouth kept twitching upward, as if she wanted to smile but had forgotten how. I knew that I had better make my move then, or I would miss my chance. So I wiped my mouth on my napkin, no longer its former pristine white but dotted with a dozen crimson stains like bloody kisses, and pushed myself out of my chair. Carol watched me get up, and the ghostly smile disappeared. She looked up at me. I waited, expecting her to say something, to ask what I had planned next, to suggest that we watch a movie or take a bubble bath. But she said nothing; instead, she kept staring right through me with those saucer eyes, deep and misty like freshwater mountain pools. Even as drunk and horny as I felt, I knew something important was happening, but I had gone too far; the wine lay over my mind like a heavy blanket, smothering my rationality and my caution, leaving only the plan. I said

You look tired, babe. Maybe I should take you to bed.

She kept staring at me for several moments, her eyes wide and unblinking. I tried to meet her gaze, but I couldn't. I had never seen her this way before, and I kept finding other places to look. Finally, she said

Michael?

and I glanced back at her, hope bursting up in my chest like heartburn. I realized to my astonishment that I wanted her to stop me, to tell me that she knew what I was up to and that she thought it was unconscionable, to yell at me like she always did when I had been stupid or insensitive. Some part of me realized that we were standing on a border, one foot in each country, and which way we decided to step was maybe the most important decision we would ever make. I wasn't up to it. I had set something in motion that I couldn't handle; it had gotten too serious when I wasn't paying attention. So when she called my name as if she were asking a question, I hoped that the right answer would come from one of us. I said

Yes, baby?

and she seemed about to speak, to give us both what we needed, the sound thinking and disciplined approach to life that she had always provided, that I had always lacked. But then she must have seen my eagerness, my need for her to be the adult, to step in and fix what I had screwed up, and she made her decision. She took a step over the border, choosing her side, and I was left standing in a country by myself, watching her watch me, seeing the resolve in her face, even though I didn't know what it meant at the time. She smiled, though her eyes didn't change, and said

Nothing.

And with that she got up and left the room, heading down the hall toward the bed and the camera and my determination to have my own way.

I took the time to grab the wine and our glasses and then followed her to the bedroom. She had already taken off her shirt and pants. She stood before me in her black bra and panties. The camera sat uncovered on its tripod, its lenscap off. She stood between it and me, hands on her hips. She indicated the camera with a toss of her head and said

This is what you wanted, right? To be here with me in front of it? I've already turned it on.

I looked from her to the camera and back again, unable to believe what I'd just heard. It was like she had come home from work and announced that she had decided to marry a parakeet and go on tour with Megadeth. She said

Go ahead and check if you don't believe me.

I was sure I'd left the camera under a blanket, as usual. I had planned to uncover it when we were good and drunk, but she had beaten me to it. The blanket lay puddled at the feet of the tripod, like one of those skirts you used to put around Christmas trees to catch the needles. I leaned around behind it and looked at the readout. The green light shone out at me like the North Star at dusk. She was telling the truth. I said

Baby, are you sure? You know we don't have to do anything you don't want to do.

Yes, I said that, and believe it or not, I meant it. You know how it is. You push and push for something until they finally give in. You've

168

outlasted them; you've won. And suddenly you feel guilty for winning, dirty for having pushed, disgusted with yourself for having to wear them down. Your triumph has finally come, and it feels cheap, like costume jewelry found half-buried in your yard. I was ready to turn off the camera and lie down next to Carol and hold her all night. But she said

Sure I'm sure. You've been after this for weeks, and you've gone to all this trouble to make it happen. If it means that much to you, we should do it.

I stared at her, speechless. It had meant a lot to me as late as that afternoon. Now something was wrong, off-kilter and slanted and hazy, but I was horny and the wine was working on me as surely as it had loosened Carol's inhibitions. She sat down on the bed and scooted up toward the headboard, leaning back on her elbows. She spread her legs and waved me forward, saying

Come on. What are you waiting for, Michael?

I didn't answer. I wished I had more time to clear my mind, to wade through all the implications and provisos. I closed my eyes and felt the room tilt to one side, and I opened them again, shaking my head. Carol had taken off her bra. I was still standing across the room, in front of the camera. It had been recording my back for perhaps a minute and a half, and part of me still wanted to turn it off. But seeing her like that, I resisted no more. I ripped off my shirt and leapt on the bed. She wrapped her arms and legs around me and squeezed me tight, the first kiss wet and sloppy, her tongue deep in my mouth. I pulled away from her, breathing hard, and as I fumbled with my pants, I saw that she was crying—not much, just one or two tears welling up in the corners of her eyes and running down her cheeks, and I just had time to wonder again if I should stop, but then she pushed me sideways and climbed on top of me, and at that point I wasn't thinking about anything at all.

I woke up late the next morning. The sun was bright and hot in the window; the clock read 10:48 AM. The other side of the bed lay empty. I raised my head from the pillow and immediately let it fall again as the hangover pain hit me like an icepick to the brain. I squeezed my eyes shut and watched the swirls and colors dance behind my lids. My mouth was bone-dry and tasted like a ten-year-old sweatsock in the bottom of someone's abandoned locker. I rubbed my temples and whispered

Shit.

I lay there for as long as I could, hoping Carol would come back to bed so that I could ask her to bring me some water and a bucket of Tylenol. But she didn't come back, so after ten minutes I staggered out of bed and toward the bathroom. I crashed shoulder first into the door frame and bounced in sideways, groaning

Goddammit.

With the light on, the bathroom was too bright; now the icepick became a pair of swords jabbed straight through my eyes. I grabbed a bottle of aspirin and the glass I always keep on the counter for just such occasions, swallowing four pills as quickly as I could. I had to stand in one place, leaning over the sink, for several moments, making sure that my stomach settled, that the aspirin stayed put. And I still hadn't seen or heard from Carol. I called out

Baby?

wincing at the sound of my voice. My head pounded like a heavy metal drum solo. Waiting for it to subside, I listened, hoping to hear even the faintest sound of movement.

Nothing.

She wasn't in the kitchen fixing breakfast or in the other bathroom taking a shower. A quick walk through the house confirmed that she wasn't in the living room or the office or the workout room. I threw on some sunglasses and poked my head out the back door. She wasn't on the deck or in the pool. I checked the driveway. Her car was gone. Aloud, I said

Maybe she went to the store for something.

It sounded lame yet perfectly plausible, and I was grasping for plausibility. This had never happened before. Regardless of what else might have been going on between us, we had always taken care of each other, and that included tending to hangovers and drink-induced injuries, like the time I separated my shoulder trying to tackle a parking meter after one too many whiskey sours. I felt a prickle of fear in my stomach, creeping its way down into my balls like a fishhook. I shivered.

Back inside, I plopped down on the couch and waited. I leaned back and closed my eyes, hoping to hear her car pulling in, her keys in the door, her voice explaining where she had gone.

Nothing.

Twenty minutes later, still alone, I remembered to check my voicemail. I rooted around until I found my cell; sure enough, there was one message. I speed-dialed my service and waited through the same old computerized voice telling me what I already knew—one new message, no saved messages. And then I heard Carol's voice, the message brief and puzzling. It said

Check the camera.

That was all.

The prickle in my stomach intensified, now more like what I imagine being stabbed with a rusty blade must feel like. I was in no condition to run, but I walked as fast as I could down the hall. I snatched the camera from the tripod and found a Post-It pinned to its screen. In Carol's handwriting, it read

Play me.

I sat down on the bed, holding the camera in my hands. Its blank screen stared back at me. I could see myself reflected in it, showing me that I looked like twenty pounds of shit in a ten-pound bag, my hair standing on end in ragged patches, stubble all over my face, my eyes wide and bloodshot. Whatever she had recorded was waiting for me. I only had to push play.

And yet I didn't. What was the point? Everything made sense now. I had pushed her too far and too often, and she had finally gotten sick of it all. She had put up with my extravagances and my blown opportunities and my bone-headed selfishness for years—missed trips, faulty products, gifts that were really for me instead of her. And just last night, I had taken something that should have been simple and fine—a meal, prepared with love; sex; tenderness; affection, and a little melancholy—and ruined it because of my schoolboy fantasy, my moment on camera that I could watch forever.

Apparently it had meant something else to her. To Carol the tape in our minds had always been enough, a memory that we could make as beautiful or as kinky or as sad as we needed. In our minds we were always young and shapely and competent, no wrinkles or bulges or knocked heads or drool. On tape, all we had was the reality, the way I stuck my elbow on her hair or how she bit my neck a bit too hard and made me yelp, or the way I belched in the middle of it all, the wine sloshing around in my stomach and threatening to burst out of me in a sad parody of orgasm. She had let me tape us to prove a point, the last one she was going to prove to me. She had taped a goodbye message and left, leaving me alone with my pounding head and shit breath for the first time since we met, her absence itself the evidence that something had changed forever.

The camera sat in my hands like a stone, heavy with possibility. I knew even then that I might be wrong, that she might have just wanted me to watch it without her to see how it turned out, that she might have left me a loving message telling me how wrong she had been, that the presence of the camera made for the best, most erotic night of her life.

And yet I couldn't shake the feeling that Carol was gone, and that whatever I had left would never be enough.

I stood up and walked slowly through my house, looking at all the things that I'd accumulated over the years. Computers with flat-screen monitors and all-in-one printers, wireless keyboards, wireless mouse. Cellular telephone with Internet connection, picture messaging, unlimited texting, whole-song ringtones. DVD system, and Blu-Ray player and HD-TV, and enough DVDs to last two lifetimes of lonely weekends and late nights. Furniture, clothes, appliances, cars. An oak deck and a pool and landscaped yard. The fruits of my labors, the evidence of my success, everything silent.

I sat in my easy chair and put up the footrest, placing my cell within reach, just in case Carol called to tell me where she was, to ask if I needed anything. I knew that if she phoned, I'd tell her that what I needed most was to hear the sound of her tires on gravel, her tread on the driveway, her voice carrying through my house until I saw her walking into the room.

The camera lay in my hands, its blank screen like the closed eye of an unconscious drunk, waiting on me to make up my mind. But really, I had only one option. I turned on the camera and pressed play, and I watched us having sex, waiting for the climax so that I could see what happened next.

www.ingramcontent.com/pod-product-compliance
Lightning Source LLC
Chambersburg PA
CBHW031236260626

47169CB00007B/2318